THEY ARE ONLY MEN

ZACHARY R. CORMIER

To family and friends, thank you.

Print ISBN: 9781790409334

PART I – SENIOR (SAMUEL)

CHAPTER 1 – THE WITNESS

Senior and Jean sat at the kitchen table in the quiet of the early morning. The sun had risen within the hour and provided the kitchen with a gentle light. Senior was dressed in his sheriff uniform with his cowboy hat resting on the table next to an empty plate with leftover scraps of eggs and potatoes. He leaned back in the chair and held the newspaper out in front of him. His bifocals rested down on the edge of his nose. He looked down through them at an angle as he read. Every minute or so he would give a gruff "hmm" from down in his throat in an unconscious manner. He sipped coffee from a large mug, which left a residue at the bottom of his thick, greyed mustache.

Jean sat across the table in her robe reading from the Bible. She would stop every so often to pray a word to the Lord.

"Says here the town council is looking for works from local artists for that renovated bus station they almost got finished," Senior said, not having looked away from the paper.

"Uh huh."

"I know one such artist that fits the bill."

"Nobody's paying for my paintings Samuel."

Senior smiled to himself, still not looking away from the paper, "I didn't say that they was paying."

Jean shook her head with a short smile and continued to read. The phone hanging on the wall rang. Jean finished the sentence she was reading and got up and walked to the wall and picked it up.

"Hello? ... Well good morning sheriff. Good to hear from you, been a long time. ... Yeah, he's sitting right here, you caught him before he headed out, hold on." Jean looked to Senior, "another one of you old sheriffs is on the phone."

"Well, is it one of the smart ones? Or is it that kind set only on causing me more headaches than I got?"

"I never met the first kind."

Senior set down the paper and headed over and took the phone from her. "Pay her no mind," Senior said into the phone.

"Sam, glad I caught you. How are you?"

"Just fine John. Until you tell me otherwise."

"Yeah, well, I ain't one for social calls."

"I know. Shoot," Senior said.

"We got something of a situation here involving a lady from your parts."

"Who's that?"

"Do you know a Helena Campos? And her daughter Lucille?"

"I know the former more than the latter. Sweet old gal. She all right?"

"Yes and no. Her daughter, that's Lucille, came down from Albuquerque yesterday to your town to pick her up and drive her back up there to see the grandkids. They left after supper, after dark, and drove back up through here. Well they were driving somewhere out near marker 230, out there in the middle of that desert, when Ms. Helena says she saw a hitchhiker out on the side of the road, an

2

older fella she says, and as they were driving just by she said she saw something up and snatch him from the dark and rush him off."

Senior stared at the wall. "Something?"

"She didn't see nothing, just the older fella snatched off quick like he had been pulled off by something at a great speed out into the dark. That's how she keeps referring to it, 'something,' she keeps saying."

"What does the daughter say?"

"She didn't see a thing. Didn't even see the man as they were driving by. Says Ms. Helena just started hollering. She pulled the car right over and got out and looked back. Yelled out a few times. But she didn't hear nothing either. Just quiet out there."

"Hmm."

"I sent a couple of my guys out there last night, and then again at first light, and they looked up and down that five-mile stretch and didn't find a thing. Nothing left behind. Nothing to speak of at all."

"And the daughter –"

"Lucille," the man said.

"Lucille. She sure she didn't see this hitchhiker?"

"Sam, she sounds about as positive as could be. She was driving and was paying attention she says and saw nothing. Though she's spooked."

"Shit, spooks me just hearing about it."

"Yeah, well."

Jean was looking on at Senior. "Who you talking about?" she asked Senior.

"Helena Campos," Senior said to her.

"She okay?"

Senior nodded to her.

"What else did the daughter say?" Senior asked the man.

"Well... hold on." There was a pause for a few moments. "Sorry about that, had to close the door there. They came on back from the restroom and are sitting just outside. Well, Ms. Lucille says that she has been concerned about her momma showing some signs of the dementia. It's something runs in the family. Says the family up there in Albuquerque was planning on sitting her down this weekend to talk her into moving up there."

"Hmm," Senior responded under his breath in his graveled tone.

"Sam. Reason I'm calling is that Ms. Helena says she isn't leaving until you come up here and take a look. She says she knows we think she's crazy, and that's okay she says, but that she's got an obligation to make sure this gets seen through."

"Hmm."

"I'm telling you, she's serious as the dead, and is growing something ornery out in the sitting room there with my deputies. You think you can at least talk to her on the phone here? Calm her down some."

Senior thought a moment. "Marker 230, what's that, twenty miles from the last service station?"

"I'd bet more," the man said.

"Long way for a hitchhiker to be out there."

"There ain't no hitchhiker," the man said.

Senior thought, turning and looking out the kitchen window at the other side of the room. That open desert out beyond the horizon.

4

"Can I call her in here so you can talk her down?" the man asked.

"Yessir," Senior said. "Put her on."

Senior could hear the man open his door and call the women into his office. Senior heard the voice of the older woman asking the man where she should sit and him saying there is only one place to sit and them settling down.

"Sam?" the man asked.

"John."

"Okay now. I got you on speaker here, you hearing everything all right?"

"Yessir."

"I got Ms. Helena here now, sitting right here okay. Ms. Helena you can go ahead and say hello."

"Sheriff?" Helena asked in her soft and worn voice. "Sheriff, you hear me?"

"Hear you just fine Helen. Heard you all had quite a night."

"Sheriff, I tell you, I saw it. Saw it plain. He tell you about it?"

"He did Helen. Told me all about it."

"Sheriff, don't mean to disrespect the man sitting here, but they don't believe a word I'm saying. They say they sent some men out there looking, and I don't want to call the man here a liar, but that don't mean I believe him either, not with how they've been looking at me, like I'm fit for the strait jacket."

"No one thinks you're crazy Helen."

"Yeah, well," she said.

"Can you tell me what he looked like?"

"The man walking or the thing that ran off with him?"

5

"Start with the hitchhiker Helen."

"Well I ain't ready to call him a hitchhiker, I know that's what he's been referred to, but I didn't see him with his thumb out or nothing."

"Okay."

"He just turned and looked at us as we was driving by at speed."

"Okay."

"He was an older man with white hair, which was either dirty, or still clinging to dark patches in places. His beard too. Had a long, full beard."

"Did you see what he was wearing?"

"Didn't notice what category of pants he was wearing, didn't catch my eye. Though he had on an old worn out military jacket – green, a dark green – and patches on it. I saw a big one on his shoulder as he was turning, it was a sword atop a shield, and the shield was made of colors, yellow and some others… I can't remember them."

"Anything else Helen?"

"Nothing else. That's all I saw. Saw him only five seconds."

"And how about the other man?"

"There wasn't another man."

"Okay."

"Just as we were passing, I saw the man snatched away like a doll out to the dark on the side there. His head jerked awful, arms went up to the side and he flew off."

Senior was quiet.

"No other way to describe it. Don't know how else to describe it," she said.

It drew quiet again.

"Ain't a man that grabbed him like that. Just ain't," she said again.

"Helen," Senior said. "I'll be up this morning."

With a voice filled with a great relief, she said, "Thank you Sheriff, I thank you, you a good man Sheriff, I knew you would."

"All right now, all right."

"Sorry Sheriff," she said, "sorry, you a good man though, you a good man."

"Okay. Helen, you've seen to your duty now. I want you to get back in that car with your daughter and go up and see the grandkids, you hear? Nothing left for you to do."

"Thank you Sheriff, thank you."

"Ma'am."

Senior could hear them gathering their things and the other sheriff escorting them out of the office and their voices growing quieter, and then their voices coming back and Helena telling the sheriff that she had something else to say.

"Sheriff? Sheriff?" she said.

"Still here dear."

"Sheriff, I thought I should say that I've seen that patch before, that one on the man's shoulder, the sword and shield, I don't know what it's for, but I've seen it."

"Means he might have been in Vietnam. Means I'm going looking for him."

Senior hung up the phone. He stood there looking at the wall and thinking. Jean was looking on.

"Were you going to take any of the horses out today?" Senior asked.

"I had no definite plans."

"You mind if I take the Appaloosa up north with me? Probably take her on a short ride out on the plain up there."

"What you looking for?"

"Don't know." Senior stared at Jean with the thoughts turning in his mind. "She the steadiest we got?" Senior asked.

"Heart like a mountain lion."

CHAPTER 2 – THE PLAINS

Senior parked the truck and trailer ten feet to the side of mile marker 230, out past the end of the shoulder, where the desert ground began again. He walked a short ways out and looked around. Rolling dirt plain with beargrass and buttes and mesas standing up off the desert floor intermittently out into the distance. The waves of heat under that summer sun were visible and rising off on the plain. The wind, which would arise here and there, was hot and dry. Senior licked at the sides of his mouth, parched and cracking from such wind and such heat. He thought on the story he had heard. From a woman who would not lie. Not to anybody.

Senior got the horse out of the trailer and walked her around a bit to get her back comfortable with him and with what was around her. She looked out with those silver-dollar eyes of a deep black, taking in this new place. Then he let her stand still for a bit and breathe and think. As Senior saddled her, he spoke to her in a soft tone about why he had brought her to this place. Her breathing calmed and her eyes grew still. He told her they were now to begin.

He rode her slow out on the dirt just off the side of the highway, starting at the mile marker sign and heading north. He scanned the ground from the blacktop to some thirty feet out upon the dirt at the beginnings of the desert and then back again as the horse walked at this plodding pace. Senior would stop the horse every so often and steer towards a spot for further inspection, and stare at that spot, and think, and then move along. Senior rode the horse three miles up the highway before he stopped and turned her around, following the same course back to the spot from which they began. When they made it back to the mile marker and the truck, Senior stopped her and turned her so that they could look back over the ground that they had covered and then covered again.

Senior looked out down the highway to the empty horizon and thought. He leaned his weight to the side and reached to the back pocket of his pants and retrieved a can of tobacco. He packed the can and got a thick pinch and filled his lower lip. He bit his lip and sucked the bitter juices until the familiar burn from under his lip arose and then he spat down to the side on the ground. He looked back out on that road and that earth.

"You see anything?"

The horse looked straight and stayed quiet.

"Yeah."

Senior looked to their side, out upon the desert plains. Like looking out at the ocean from its shore. And all that endless space looking back. And the soft, timeworn song calling to them, as it has to many it has swallowed since the beginning. He nodded, feeling small.

"It don't feel so empty as it looks, huh?" Senior asked, still looking out. "What do you think that is? Something within or something without?"

The horse turned herself toward the open land. As the horse settled, she pointed the two of them toward one particularly large mesa head four or five miles out. As Senior stared out upon it, it seemed to resemble something like a tall gravestone standing forth of a radiant crimson from the sun shining down upon it. Though it appeared at least slightly taller than any other structure out upon the plain, there was something else about it that drew attention. A heaviness to the thing.

"I see it," Senior said. "What you thinking?"

The horse made something of a groan down deep in her throat.

"Hold on," he said. "I'll get the gun."

Senior rode the horse slow across the plain toward this mesa standing tall out ahead. The double-barrel shotgun was loaded and resting across his lap as he guided her on. Though Senior was aware that most all feelings from the world about are cast upon the scene from what a person was conjuring up themselves, he did feel a pull from that monument before them which did not emanate from any of the other structures out on this plain. All others inanimate and this thing alive. He continued to scan the desert floor before them, panning left and then right and then left again.

The horse saw it first and stopped. It then caught Senior's eye. There was a small black object out straight ahead on the path to the mesa. Some item upon the ground. They both stood there still and looking at it. "Come on," he said, nudging the horse forward. The horse was hesitant and turned her head. Senior leaned forward and patted the side of her long neck. A smooth and warm skin. He whispered easy, "It's why we came." He nudged her on, and after a moment, she moved forward.

Senior stopped her ten feet short of the object and got down. It was a worn-out cowboy boot of a dark leather that bore some darker stains with some even darker stain streaked across the dirt behind. Senior stared at it. He looked around the scene for anything else but found nothing.

Senior set the shotgun down on the ground. He walked to the boot and then stood staring down at it. He knew the streaks on the ground were blood, caking that dirt there like a filthy syrup. He looked down into the boot with the sun shining in from directly above and there was some dark substance down in it as well which did bear a blackened hue of the blood. He exhaled and bent down and took hold of the boot and picked it up.

There was a heaviness to it that made his stomach hurt. He smelled a rot and did not bring the boot any closer to his face, but held it down by his waist. Senior removed his knife from his belt and flipped the blade open. He held the boot out and stabbed into the rear of the boot and then jerked the blade upwards, tearing the soft leather of the boot's rear. Senior exhaled again and then inserted the fingers of both his hands into this opening, getting a grip, and then tore the two sides of the opening as far as he could down to the sole. He turned the opening at the back of the boot over to face the earth and began shaking it so as to drop the boot's contents upon the ground.

The foot fell out of the boot and dropped upon the desert floor with a thud. Though Senior had made such conclusion already, the sight of the thing sent his heart up into his throat, with him flinching awful and hollering out under his breath as he jumped back and turned away from it. He made sounds something like clearing his throat as he paced like a man that had stubbed his toe. The horse stared the severed appendage down curious from its short distance away.

Senior put both hands upon his hips and looked up at the sky. "Lord," he said. He stood there shaking his head.

He looked back to it with a sorry expression. It was a bare foot of a white skin that was bruised and bloated. The foot was snapped off clean just above the ankle, bearing some bone in the middle of the open wound with mangled flesh about it. Each of the toes were swollen and distorted, though they wore the black toe nails still.

Senior cleared his throat again and looked out over the plain and shook his head more. He thought over the mechanics which could have led to such a result with the boot still intact and concluded only that there was some foreign force behind it of a sinister physics. He looked to the horse, who was still staring at the thing. She then looked to him and kept looking at him, waiting.

Senior turned back around again, looking out past the mess upon the earth, and stared at the mesa head in the short distance. He thought on it. He thought about what his obligations might have been in the moment, and to whom such obligations were owed, both in a lateral and vertical sense.

Senior walked back to the horse, looking down at the earth as he came. When he reached the horse, he bent down and retrieved the shotgun. He stood holding it in his hands. In the company of the evidence upon the ground behind him, the gun seemed a feeble thing, as did whatever was within himself. He looked to the horse's eye, an orb of wet obsidian staring on and measuring the man.

"Choice was made when we came out here," he said to her. As she continued to look, blinking at him, he thought to himself that such choice was actually made long before, as such decisions are just overflow from what a person has become.

Senior patted the horse's neck. He turned and looked again at that tall, burnt mesa standing forth from the earth. "It ain't my jurisdiction. But He has all the jurisdictions in His hand and we His tools alike."

Senior got back atop the horse and rode along with the shotgun again cradled upon his lap, with him seeing the foot and the blood and the boot out in his periphery, though he gave them not a look.

They reached a point some fifty yards from the base of the mesa and its mighty face stretching up above and looking down upon them. Senior looked the thing over from top to bottom, the jagged and chaotic edges of its coarse skin wearing many shades of crimson and maroon and adobe and a dark pink of the epochs. An ancient and beautiful thing looking down upon this small and untimely speck before it. The rock faces that could be seen all up and down bore no opening or imperfection within which to hide. "Come on," Senior said, pulling the reins to his side and steering the horse to a path in such direction to walk the mesa's circumference and learn all her faces.

Senior rode slow and scanned the mesa from its top down to its bottom and upwards again before moving his sight to the right and beginning again. Senior kept the horse walking straight as they continued to circumnavigate the thing, approaching slowly to its rear, or at least what Senior thought of as the rear from the direction which they had approached.

Not long after they had reached the backside of the mesa, Senior found the imperfection which he had been looking for. Down at the base of the mesa where it met the desert floor was the dark mouth of an opening into which shadow was thrown from where the noon sun hung above. Senior stopped the horse and stared at the opening. The rim of the opening was of a rugged line and appearing of a natural origin. "You see it there?" He asked the horse. "Take me just there." He kicked at her sides gentle, but firm, and she began to approach.

The mouth of the opening stood ten feet high. Senior looked into the opening from fifteen feet out atop the horse. The light allowed him only to see that the floor and ceiling of the tunnel sloped rather sharply downwards into the darkness. There was nothing on the ground in front of the opening. Senior put his fingers into his lip and grabbed at the dried wad of tobacco and took it out and threw it upon the ground. He swabbed underneath his lip with his tongue and gathered the remaining particles and spat them down to the dirt. He got down from the horse.

Senior unfastened the loop of rope from the rear of the saddle and untied it free. He tied the far end of the rope around the base of a boulder which leaned against the mesa wall with a clove-hitch knot and then tied a bowline and then another on the other end of the fifty-foot rope at the halter underneath the horse's jaw. The horse stood some twenty feet to the side of the opening. Senior pet her down along the bridge of her face to her snout and told her not to leave him there alone.

Senior took hold of the shotgun and walked back to the opening with intent to step quietly. He stopped directly in front of it and stood looking into the dark. He listened. There was only quiet down the tunnel and there was only quiet beside him up on the earth. He had ventured down into caverns beneath like-mesas before. He had brought his

15

boys those many years ago. They had once found a deposit of arrowheads halfway down to the bottom of one such tunnel forged from quartzite stones by some Mescalero Apache ancient. He thought about the faces of his boys. One now a man, and the other a memory, which will remain that of a boy until seen again in the kingdom. Could he see his daddy now? What does he say to him?

Senior took hold of the long aluminum issue flashlight upon his belt with one hand and removed it and pointed it at the center of the opening and clicked it on. The sunlight on the surface would not allow the beam to be seen but something of a dim ring out in the dark. But as he walked into the mouth of the tunnel, such ring focused in the dark, and once he was within the mouth, and with the dark enveloping him entire, the body of the beam appeared stretching out to the ring at its end. The air was a sudden cold and stale upon his face. Senior took a short piece of rope from the back of his belt and used it to fasten the flashlight in between the barrels of the shotgun pointing forward. Once it was tight, Senior tested it by pointing the gun out into the dark like a headlight. Senior held the shotgun firm in both hands and pointed the beam down the tunnel. Senior crept forward and downward as if with plans of sneaking up upon a sleeping ghost.

CHAPTER 3 – UNDER THE EARTH

The tunnel narrowed both at his sides and above him as he made his way down the slope. There was no color in this kind of dark, but only a lifeless hue of gray from the flashlight. The roof dropped down to around seven feet, with the walls on each side coming likewise inward to just a few feet from him. Senior's throat tightened in like fashion and he resisted the urge to clear it as was otherwise his custom as keeping the quiet was the singular thought which consumed his mind. The floor of the tunnel downward was a rugged rolling stone surface, with some large stone blocks about which needed to be side-stepped or otherwise stepped-over with caution. He continued downward at the slowest of paces.

It was two or three minutes before he reached the end of the descent, having traveled some fifty yards down into the earth. The narrow tunnel opened before him into an expanse which he saw was a large cavern. Senior scanned the floor of the cavern with the dull beam. The room stretched a great distance out ahead and to his sides, with the differing shapes of variously sized stones standing all about the floor, many much taller than him. Senior turned the beam upwards to the cavern's ceiling, which could not be discerned, floating high above somewhere in the black. Senior was surprised at how cold it was here.

There came a soft groan from the floor of the cavern out ahead. Senior snapped the beam back down to level out toward where the sound had originated. His heart rose to a hammer. A heat grew from within and raised the temperature inside his head to where his ears began to

17

tingle with a hotness at their rims.   He stood still and listened.

And there came another groan, deeper in tone, from an entirely different direction out in the dark. Senior turned the beam quickly towards it. The many stones standing tall upon the cavern floor cast shadows from the beam like a hundred phantoms out ahead. Such shadows played tricks upon his eyes as the fear gripped his perception of the scene. He was locked in place and listening.

"What would bring an old man down to this place?" said the voice of a man somewhere out in the dark in a deep tone, echoing, and holding in the air and fading.

"Chance does not exist here. Not here," the voice said, again echoing and drawing out over the cavern.

"And alone?" the voice asked, now from a completely different direction across the other side of the cavern, still hidden in the shadows and the dark, reaching this other location with a speed that put a still to Senior's heart. Senior swung the point of the shotgun and flashlight to this other area from which the voice had now come. Senior still could see nothing, except for those shadows rising off the large standing stones and looking down upon him in their lifeless forms.

"But you're not alone. Are you? What is it you have there?" There was the sound like something scampering fast over the rock floor toward the other direction. Senior followed such sound quick as he could with the point of his light and gun. But still, he saw nothing.

"What could such a thing do for you here? It betrays you."

"You killed that man?" Senior called out steady.

"I've killed many. Can't you feel them?" the voice asked, now again from another side to Senior, but closer. Like there was no body to him, but only a presence, which could fill any part of this place. Senior knew that wasn't true, that there was a body out there, which fact frightened him more than the previous thought.

"Today's the day then," Senior said. It was quiet. The quiet hung for a very long moment. The pain in Senior's chest rose by the second. "You don't have to die. Come out here where I can see you and I'll take you in alive. Promise you."

It was quiet again. And from an entirely different spot to Senior's side, again the man called in something more like a whisper, "You will never leave this place."

The great cavern drew silent once more. Senior listened for anything out in the dark as he slowly scanned the beam across the cavern floor ahead. His eyes were wide and he held his breath.

There was something like a scratching out from his side. Senior jerked the point of the gun over towards this sound and saw the flash of some form speeding toward him in a rush only feet away – the shotgun burst as the flame from the barrels covered this form in that second – a shriek broke out from this form – and Senior fell backwards to the ground on his rear both from the force of the gun and the startle from the sudden sight of the thing. The thunder from the gun rolled outwards and then upwards along the cavern walls, followed by the high pitch from the scream, and the two blended and faded as Senior picked himself up to sitting and struggling to point the beam and the gun back where he had seen it.

There was a body ten feet out ahead on the ground. From it came a sound something like a struggle to breathe. The thing was chest down, but slowly pushing itself upwards. Senior locked the beam of the flashlight upon it. The thing raised its head up, showing the face of a man with long black hair hanging wildly about, his face filled with a pain and a fury.

Senior felt frantically about his belt for the pouch which held the shells. He found it and groped within for some seconds – the sound of some other shells falling out and rattling on the stone floor. He got a hold on two and took them out. He broke the gun open, taking the beam off the man, loaded the shells, snapped it together, and cocked it. He returned the beam to the man's face, who was now crawling toward him with mouth open and baring his teeth as if a beast. Senior pulled the trigger, and in the jolt backward from the kick and roar of the gun, Senior saw the man's head whip backward, with the man rolling away and falling still. This explosion again filled the cavern, rolling heavy and then fading above.

Senior sat still on his rear holding the beam and barrel point fixed upon the body. It was not moving. Senior struggled for breath, his chest heaving, asthmatic and out of control. The wheeze at the top of the forced breaths was loud and his nose was giving a snort upon him sucking air back in. The body was not moving.

"Easy," Senior said at the top of an inhale. "Easy," he said again a few short breaths later. A chant his mother used to soothe him as a child during such an onset. "Easy," he said. "Easy." Over the next minute he gained more control over the breath. That heavy feeling pulling back from the center of his chest. Senior kept the light upon the body. Still no movement.

Senior leaned to his side and pushed himself up onto one knee and then onto both and then pushed himself up to standing with a sharp pain coming from his lower back and with his knee cracking. "Ah, shit," he said under a stifled breath and grimace.

He stepped forward and stood over the man. The man was lying face down, with black hair sprawled out and covering his head. The man was wearing jeans, but was barefoot. He had on a dark t-shirt. Senior leaned down and took hold under the man's armpit and turned him over. The man's t-shirt was torn apart at the chest from the first shot. When Senior got the light back upon the man's face his stomach turned. The man's face was caved inward and deformed from the impact of the buckshot.

Senior looked away and got hold of that heaviness in his throat and looked back to what had been the man's face.

A man. Of a native people to this land it seemed from the tan of the skin. The man's mouth was agape and his eyes shut. A man he thought. A man. The quiet seemed now empty of that heaviness which had pressed down upon him before.

Senior then noticed something. At first it was so slight that it was almost indiscernible. It grew though upon the man's face in those seconds, a tremble, but not of the entire structure of what had been the head, but only of the skin. And Senior found himself holding his breath again as he noticed that there was no blood. No lacerations. The whole of the thing was caved inwards, but there had been no penetrations.

Senior knelt down and brought himself in close. His mind had mostly come back together from the shock of it all. Such blast should have blown the man's head clear off. But there it was.

The tremble atop the skin grew in its slow, but gradual momentum. It seemed a substance was running underneath. Senior looked close as he could and saw progress from within, like something filling in the facial structures. Senior watched this progress for two minutes from his position close to the man's face. He then leaned back a bit and saw it from a wider angle. It could not be denied. The face of the man was pushing itself back together from within.

Senior pointed the light and gun back to the man's chest. The chest exposed through the torn shirt also was without any blood.

Senior stood up. The familiar pain awoke in his heart again and began to throb. He pointed the gun back to the man's face and watched in the soft light this advance continue and gain greater progress for the next five minutes. Like watching those videos of grass growing in fast motion. Senior broke the shotgun open and released the two shells. Senior reached into the pouch at the back of his belt and retrieved two more. The man's face was approaching restoration. Senior loaded each of the shells, steadied the gun, and waited. Another three or four minutes went by in the quiet.

The man's lips began to move as that open mouth drew very slowly to a close and then tightened. The man's eyes opened. Dark, full pupils surrounded by another ring of black. And the man's face slowly turned until the man was looking directly up at Senior.

Senior shot him directly between the eyes at this point blank range, whipping the man's head over to the side awful. The man did not make a sound and returned to a dead still. The acrid stench of the burnt propellant rose through Senior's nostrils.

Senior stepped forward again. He used the edge of the barrels to turn the man's head back toward him. It was caved in again at its center, with a similar dent inwards on the temple. Senior knelt down again and watched.

After a long minute, he saw again that tremble begin, ever so slight, but again increasing from this starting point as it had before. Senior stood up. This vast cavern felt in a sudden tight about him like a coffin. Disjointed thoughts and options raced in his mind. Senior cleared his throat. He began to feel about his belt at the objects that were fastened to it and hanging. He came to that smaller pouch holding the cuffs, with his hand stopping and holding still. He opened the pouch with his free hand and removed the two sets of handcuffs. He held them there, looking at them.

Senior stepped forward and knelt back down. He saw this tremble beginning to show the slow signs of progress again upon the smashed contours of the man's face. Senior put down the gun completely and used both hands to roll the man over onto his stomach. He found the man's right wrist and secured the cuff tight as he could upon it. He found the man's left wrist and brought it across the man's back and clamped the other cuff down secure. Senior then scooted down the man's legs to his feet. Senior took the man's right ankle within his hand and cuffed it, clamping the cuff together with all his strength. Senior then took the other cuff and squeezed it closed upon the other ankle. Senior leaned back and looked down upon the result, the man's hands cuffed behind his back and his feet cuffed tightly together.

Senior thought more. He looked back to the gun. He moved for it and took it back within his hands and began to go to work at untying the flashlight from in between the barrels of the gun. Senior set the flashlight down upon the floor at an angle to cast light upon his task. Senior took the rope and leaned back over to the man. Senior positioned himself below the man's feet and took both feet within his hands and pushed them upwards towards the man's hands cuffed behind his back, bending the man's knees as he went. When the feet went as far as the bends of the knees would allow, Senior put the shin of his leg down across them with his weight driving the heels of the feet down into the man's hamstrings. Senior then began tying the cuffed feet tight to the cuffed hands, hogtieing the man. Senior tied three opposing knots down tight, using every last bit of the rope.

Senior stepped back, picked up the flashlight, and reviewed his work. The man lay prostrate upon his chest, with his hands and feet tied down fast and meeting upon his rear. If this process ran the same course, he had something like ten minutes before the thing awoke. No man could free himself from such a position. None. He did not know the strength of the thing, but he could not believe that it could snap the rope and steel bands of the cuffs behind its back. There was no leverage for it.

Senior gave himself one minute to think. He could leave the thing here. Just leave him. It would take him several hours to return with other men. That would be painful time. This thing was now his charge. And the weight of it could not be discerned, though he felt some great multitude of pain and death emanating from the thing lying there, a dark relic with history sprawling unknown, with a thousand past-afflicted souls crying out to him from behind the wall, of the anomaly of the moment and its fading hope for a justice, if such a thing was possible.

Senior picked up the shotgun with his other hand and walked to the man's side. He knelt down and threaded the barrel of the shotgun through the opening behind the bend of the man's knees. Senior turned back and held out the flashlight to show the path upon which he would have to drag the man back to the tunnel, which was forty or so feet away. Senior took inventory of such scene in his mind. Senior looked back to the body. He set the flashlight upon the ground and turned it to cast what light it could upon the path behind him. He took hold of the shotgun with both hands gripping at opposing spots just outside the bent knees of the man, using the gun like a bar he could pull upon to drag the man backwards. Senior tightened his grip, took a breath, raised himself upon his feet in a hunched over position, and then began shuffling backwards.

CHAPTER 4 – TAKING HIM

Once the motion began, the man was not altogether heavy in this drag. Senior grunted as he continued to shuffle backwards quickly. He committed to making it to the mouth of the tunnel leading upwards before he would stop to take a breath. After a half-minute of dragging the man, Senior looked backwards over his shoulder and found that he was just arriving at the tunnel. He stopped and let the man's legs fall to the floor, though he continued to hold the barrel of the gun with both hands. He took several breaths and then looked back again and up the tunnel. There at its top so far away was an orb of light. He must be in that light when the man awoke, when this thing awoke. Whatever might be at stake depended upon it.

Senior pushed out three short breaths as if a countdown and began dragging the thing up the tunnel. The thing's body was light no longer. Senior could not help but to grunt with each exhale, every step an isolated war against his will followed by another and another in the climb. Senior's mantra internal – you cannot lose one step, you cannot lose one step. It was absolute dark in the tunnel. Senior could not see the body and could not see himself, or the ground being covered. Senior stumbled several times as the backs of his heels struck various stones and edges of the floor. He could only regain balance and keep on with the pull, with no time for technique or care, forcing this deadweight over every obstacle with vicious tugs when needed. Senior's grunts and cries and breaths were loud and filled the dark of the tunnel echoing. Every muscle in his legs burned. His shoulders burned. His hands burned.

Everything weakening. His head grew light in the disorienting struggle. His fear shifted from the failing muscles to passing out and rolling down the slope and waking up to who knows what, if he awoke at all. It was true torture through the minutes. Though in the midst of the noise about and within, he perceived some song inaudible which carried him.

The daylight and the leveling of the ground beneath him was a sudden thing. Senior shuffled still several feet upon the open desert floor before it was realized and then he collapsed and released all. The sun was an overwhelming spotlight peering down upon him and forcing his eyes to close. The baked air was a burn in his lungs. His calves cramped with spasms. His forearms cramped as well and crooked his hands over his wrists. He laid, accepting such pain, alive and in the light.

Senior rolled to his side and opened his eyes. The man was five feet away, lying on his side upon the dirt – his eyes open and staring back. The man was still bound with both hands and feet tight behind him. He did not struggle, or move in any way. He just stared into Senior's eyes. Something of surprise and admiration. Senior did not break the stare and looked back to those eyes, the exhaustion still not allowing him to move.

But the fear did begin to arise within Senior that if he did not pick himself up now, he may never do so. His throat ached with dryness. Senior received again the agony which came with pushing himself to his knees and then to standing. He wobbled there for a moment and looked around for the horse. There she was, right where he had left her tied to the rock, standing still and blinking at him from the short distance.

Senior stumbled within a quick pace to the horse. When he reached her, he leaned against her and caught his breath again. He felt around the saddle until he found the canteen. He unscrewed the lid and let it fall without care to the ground and poured the water down his throat without any more care, much of it running down his cheeks and chin and neck, though it all felt and tasted like some paradise. Senior held the canteen up at this angle for several seconds even after it no longer produced. He then let it fall to the ground as well.

Senior looked back at the man lying on the ground. The man had not moved and continued to lay still. Looking at him.

"That's him," Senior said to the horse. The horse stared at the man lying upon the ground out in the short distance.

"I don't know what we're into here. But we're in all the way. Understand?"

The horse looked back at him without change.

"Okay then."

Senior walked to the large rock to which the horse was tied. He knelt down at the base of the rock and found the knots holding it fast. He bit down upon his lip and fought through more of the pain in his locked fingers and hands as he worked at untying these knots. When free, he pulled the rope to himself until its end was in hand. He stood up and returned to the horse. He looked into her eye there on the side of her head and patted her neck. "Like a lion."

Senior walked the horse toward the man lying still on the ground. The man only watched them approach. Senior expected some struggle from him to test what was binding him and the lack of such efforts was unnerving. As was his silence and his calculating. Senior stopped walking about ten feet out and patted the horse's snout until she stopped and understood to stay still upon the spot.

The shotgun lay on the ground halfway between where Senior stood and where the man lay. The man did not look at it, but only kept looking up at Senior's face. Senior took the end of the rope with him and stepped to the gun and bent down and picked it up. Senior gave the man a look, a statement of what it meant that Senior again had the gun within his hands. Senior reached into the pouch on his belt and found the last two shells. He broke the gun open and loaded each of the shells and closed the gun again and cocked it. Senior gave the man this look again.

"I'm coming to your feet there and I'm tying the end of this rope to you."

The man's stare was not affected.

"You move but a muscle and I'll drop you again. Understand?"

A thin smile spread across the man's face. Senior raised the barrel in line with the man's face and held it there.

"I was planning on saving these. Maybe it'd be easier if I didn't."

The man's smile remained a few moments and then faded. The quiet between them settled into place.

Senior cleared his throat dryly and spat what he could down upon the ground to his side. "Okay."

Senior kept the gun pointed at the man's face as he stepped past the man and then behind the man, who was still laying upon his side. Senior knelt down and threaded the end of the rope through and around the man's bent knees at the same spot within which he had braced the barrel of the gun to drag him up to the earth. Senior tied the rope secure with opposing knots. The man lay still during this process. Senior put speculation as to the reason for this out of his mind. Whatever such reasoning, it would do him no good to think on it, as there was but one path before him out of this desert, and with this thing dragging behind him, his wretched prize and prisoner.

Senior kept the horse at a slow walk as they drug the man behind them at the end of the rope some twenty feet back. Senior looked over his shoulder and kept his eyes on the man with the gun in hand. Being drug in this hogtied position by the legs, with chest flat on the ground, the man arched his back and neck to keep his face from being drug across the ground. The man faced the other direction behind them, with his long dark hair shrouded about his head and shoulders. Senior pictured his face still devoid of emotion or feeling. Senior was afraid if he made the thing too uncomfortable it might give up its patient act and show its true strength in trying what bound it. They gradually left the great mesa head behind them, with it looking down upon them stoically, reserving its judgment of these strange pilgrims within its primordial silence.

The horse spotted the truck and trailer out ahead distant on the plain and kept a trajectory straight for them without needing Senior's guidance. Senior was without a plan and one was not coming together. Since he was a boy, he had found himself only comfortable in the truth and the path it laid before it. But at the intersection of these worlds come together, there were deeper truths and obligations to be calculated, of which most men could not perceive, much less acknowledge. What would he say if a man showed up at his station with another man bound this way and his only explanation something which could not be credited without casting all aside. People do not believe in evil. Not really. Because what else would such a belief require? No. People do not want to believe in anything, lest they have to believe in everything. It is a thing for the ancients, the so called ignorants. Though Senior wondered what words they might have for this generation. At least they knew themselves. Wherever he was going, he was going alone. To invite others would be to invite their suppositions, which would be to invite their waiting destruction, accelerated. All a person's life is a test. Senior knew this thing and him were brought together through probabilities unthinkable for this very decision. Would he cower? Would he dare to judge the thing proper? Would he fear what was within himself, and what this thing might try to coax from him? Would he do what was required?

The horse walked right up to the back of the trailer until its wet nose pushed against the rear wall, as if it were a thing trained. The man tied behind came to a stop and rolled onto his side and looked at them. Senior stared him down. He stepped down from the horse and stood staring again at the man out on the ground. Senior put the gun down on the ground and went to untying the rope from the rear of the saddle. He let it drop to the ground beside the gun. Senior unsaddled the horse and set the saddle upon the ground. Senior would look to the man every few moments. The man did not move. He just laid still, looking on.

Senior got his keys and opened the trailer door and walked the horse inside the trailer. He got her up to the front of the trailer and fastened the leather strap hanging from the wall to her halter ring. Senior patted her just behind her ears.

Senior walked out and shut the trailer. He locked it again. Senior kept his eyes upon the man as he walked over to the driver's door of the truck and opened it and stepped up and in, leaving the door open to his side. Senior used another key on his chain at the base of a panel that ran along the top of the front bench seat, which popped free the top of the cage divider to isolate the rear cab. He raised the cage divider up to the roof of the cab and snapped it in place and locked it again. It had been at least a couple years since he had personally detained and transported anyone. Senior pulled on the cage divider to ensure that it was locked secure. He sat back down and turned and looked at the man from his seated position in the truck. The man was lying on his side in the same position, with his head resting on the dirt. The man looked not worried in the slightest. Senior stepped out of the cab. He opened the rear driver's side door all the way and left it.

Senior walked back to the gun and picked it up. The man's eyes followed him. Senior stood there looking at the man with the gun in his hands.

"Time to go," he said. The man did not respond.

Senior walked the line of the rope laying on the ground between them until he stood a few feet from the man.

"I haven't decided what to do with you yet," Senior said.

"Yes you have."

"You got steel cuffs on your wrists and ankles. You feel them?"

"I do."

"I'm going to cut that rope binding them together. I prefer not to have to shoot your ass and drag you over and throw you in the truck there, but I will."

The man looked at the gun in Senior's hands and then looked back to his eyes.

"Okay then," Senior said.

Senior walked around the man down by his feet and went and kneeled down behind him. He took hold of the barrel of the gun in one hand and used the other to retrieve the knife from his belt. He opened the blade and began sawing at the rope just beneath the first knot. The rope broke in a sudden and the man's feet and legs snapped down to the ground, startling Senior and sending him up onto his feet and backing away while raising the gun upon the man. But the man just laid there.

"Get up."

The man's hands were still cuffed tightly behind his back, with his ankles also still cuffed, with the chain between the cuffs stretching four inches taut. The man slid his butt backward as he moved himself to a kneeled position. Senior pointed the gun square at the back of the man's head. The man secured his base beneath him, spreading his feet apart as far as the chain on the cuffs about his ankles would allow, and rose himself slowly to standing, again wobbling slightly, and then finding his balance. The man remained facing toward the truck and away from Senior, who still stood five feet behind him.

"Go on."

The man turned his head and looked at Senior. This is what you want, the man appeared to be asking. Senior gestured with the point of the gun toward the truck.

The man turned his head back away and began shuffling his feet forward. Senior trailed him at the short distance all the way until the man reached the rear door of the truck, open and waiting for him. The man turned about-face towards Senior, and with a face still calm as could be, hopped up and backwards with his rear meeting with the bench seat. The man scooted himself in and turned forward. He came to rest in the seat with his hands still bound behind his back. The man drew still and looked back to Senior and waited.

Senior kept the gun pointed upon the man's face until he got to the door and reached out with one hand and pushed it shut. Senior stood there looking through the dark glass at the faded outline of the man looking back at him.

CHAPTER 5 – THE ROAD

The presence of this thing filled the quiet of the cab with a heaviness. Senior could feel the man's eyes upon the back of his head as he drove. Every minute or so, Senior would look at the rear view mirror and see him staring on. The blacks of those eyes. It stayed quiet between them for the first stretch of the drive as they made their way upon the highway.

Senior looked to the mirror again and found himself staring a bit longer at the man. If he had not so recently been through the experience, he could convince himself that this thing was only a man. A rawness to him. But overall unassuming and quiet.

"Why are you letting this happen?" Senior finally asked.

The man stared on for a moment longer. "Curious, I guess."

"No sense in that," Senior said, looking at the man again upon the mirror. "Usually means it's a lie."

"No man has ever come looking for me. Not ever."

"How long's ever?"

"A very long time."

Senior looked back to the road.

"Never been turned over to a man's hands either," the man said. "What do you think that means?"

Senior checked the man again in the mirror.

"Must mean something. Everything does," the man said.

The cab returned to its silence. The sound of the air through the vents. The road.

"Depends entirely upon what kind of man you are," the man began again.

"How's that?"

"You could have run. Left this all behind you. Like most all men would. But you chose what was unthinkable for a man. To push this story forward with yourself still inside. There are only three reasons I can think of for that choice."

Senior looked at the man's eyes in the mirror, willing to hear this.

"Wrath. One of those souls had some connection to you and this is all as simple as you finding me out to cast that pain back upon me." The man measured the small reflection of Senior's face. "But you would have tried such torture first chance you had out there. And that kind of character doesn't live in those eyes of yours."

The conclusion sat in the air uncontested.

"Ambition. You have it in mind to make a name off of me. The man that brought the monster to the world."

Senior did not even look to the mirror at this.

"You know that could never be. They don't want to see such a thing. Do they? They deny themselves. They would deny me. They would deny you."

Senior looked only to the road.

"Or fear. You see. You are the rare soul that sees behind all that appears before him that thread upon which the whole narrative is strung together and a running back to the source."

This did draw Senior's eyes to the mirror once again.

"You're afraid," the man said, pausing, and letting this sit in the air. "Of Him."

Senior looked back to the road.

"Of being like the rest of them. As if there was no curse. As if there was no one looking on."

"What did you do with that man?" Senior asked at last, still looking at the road.

The man looked out the side window. The desert passing by.

"You eat him?" Senior asked again.

The man only continued to stare out the window. "I wonder whether you'll hold up," the man replied. "We'll see," he said in a quieter tone. The man looked to the mirror and saw Senior's eyes upon him. "Not everything has a name."

It was quiet again between them. A sign appeared ahead identifying the next town out five miles ahead. If Senior was to take the man back to the sheriff of the county, this would be his exit.

When the exit appeared up ahead, Senior began to slow the truck and eventually pulled off onto the shoulder and came to a stop. Senior pressed the button that flashed the warning lights on the back of the truck and trailer. Senior sat thinking. The clicks from the warning lights sounded every half second in their rhythm. The man studied the scene through the windshield and then he studied Senior up front. Senior stared out at the exit sign.

"Some years back, we caught up with a fella that had parked a trailer on some land out by the lake down in south county. Two teenage girls had gone missing within three months from towns around that area. Another from the reservation. It was the troopers that eventually came upon the trailer in going about talking to folks. No telling how

37

many souls through the years. He just kept moving the thing along through the country as far as we could tell. Doing what he did."

Senior turned himself in his seat and looked back through the cage at the man direct. "That man didn't say a word at the arrest. Didn't say a word the entire time locked up awaiting the trial. I met with him alone just the one time down at the jail outside of town to interview him. He wasn't talking, so I just sat there staring at him until he would. Looked right into those eyes of his there for a long time."

Senior drew quiet and sat looking at the man. "You aren't afraid of the Almighty?"

The man stared back with a glare. He held his eyes wide and still. Letting Senior have his look.

Senior turned back to looking out the windshield. He put the truck in drive and turned back onto the highway and accelerated gradually. They drove by the exit and sped down the highway towards home. It was quiet for the next hour as they drove. The man no longer stared at Senior. When Senior would check the mirror, the man was looking out the side-window at that desert world spread out before him and passing by.

They reached the long incline stretching up the hill just before town. The truck and trailer slowed all the way up the slope until they came to its top, with the town appearing out before them and at the bottom of the other side of the slope down below. The man stretched his neck upwards to see the place. The truck picked up a great momentum on the descent with the trailer behind making a whirring sound with the rush before Senior began to slow the truck with the exit coming up ahead.

They exited and drove down the off-ramp and eventually came to a stop at a stoplight. The outskirts of the small downtown and Main Street appeared a mile or so down the road ahead. A car pulled up to the left of the truck and trailer and also stopped at the light. There was a middle-aged woman alone in the vehicle. She looked over to Senior and stared at him. She looked to the back window, which was tinted, and only showing the outline of the man. Senior made a sound as if he was about to say something to the man in the back, but he stopped, and did not pick up again. The light turned green. The truck rolled slowly forward toward downtown.

The sight of the people walking on the sidewalks of Main Street stirred an anxiety within Senior. The reality of bringing the thing within proximity to them. Their faces. Faces he knew. Senior checked the man constantly in the rearview. The man was looking out the side window at these people. The man's expression was blank still and not revealing the thoughts running behind those eyes.

A red light appeared out ahead at the next stoplight. Senior turned on the blue and red flashers. The truck came to a slow roll just before the intersection. Senior pushed the siren button twice, giving two sharp chirps. All other vehicles came to a stop. Senior raised his hand in thanks and drove through the intersection. The far side of the down town area appeared out ahead. Senior picked up speed at this and made the green light for the last stoplight in the small town and continued on this road with the countryside out past the edge of town coming to view with the neighborhoods beginning again.

They drove out of the town and into the countryside, coming eventually to the country road that would lead them in some short miles to Senior's ranch home. The midafternoon sun halfway down to the horizon out ahead was still cooking. The man stared out the side-window in the quiet that had set firmly between them. Observing the homes and ranchlands. They came to a dirt road and turned onto it. The ranch homes were now further spread out by the desert land between each of them.

"Going home," the man said.

Senior did not look to the mirror. The truck swayed with the imperfections of the road, carrying the constant sound of the dirt beneath.

"You could live with me a prisoner in your home?"

Senior looked only out at the road. At the homes of the people he knew. Carrying this thing by.

"Have you considered the resolve? Truly?"

Quiet still. Senior drove on.

Senior saw his ranch a quarter mile down the road. He slowed the truck to a stop. They sat there as the truck idled. Senior thought on it. Confirming it all within himself. Senior did not look to the man as he feared he would lose his nerve. Senior looked over to the passenger seat and the shotgun. He accelerated again toward his home just there.

When they came within fifty yards of the home, Senior began to ease off the accelerator. There was a noise of some shifting from the back. Senior looked to the mirror and saw the man's hands upon the cage with fingers pushing through the gaps and gripping – the man's face appearing just behind and pressing up against the cage with

40

a wildness returned. Senior hollered out and jerked the steering wheel to the right, diverting the truck to the side of the road and then off of it.

Senior's vision was split between what was out ahead and the mirror above. The rear view mirror – the man's mouth opened wide beyond natural with teeth extending out pointed and brilliant. The windshield – the truck speeding for the telephone pole at the edge of the ranch's fence line with its thick railroad ties standing forth as posts. Everything bouncing and shaking powerfully of the rugged earth. Amidst the violent blend of sound from the force of the truck and its weight careening and skidding across the uneven land was suddenly the crack of the cage being torn from its anchors. The sight of the man pulling the cage away and dropping it from sight. The sight of the man's face backing away to let the cage drop and then rushing forward.

Senior dropped his foot upon the gas hard as he could, the engine screamed in a high pitch. As Senior clamped his hands down upon the steering wheel he felt the man's cold hands upon each of the sides of his neck and squeezing with a power rising behind them he knew would take him from the world in pieces. The thick wooden pole now at the nose of the truck. All of it happening within a breath and also as if in a still - rolling slowly for him to observe all the details of this shot of the world at the moment it would shatter.

There was the dull explosion of the crash and an abrupt dark and a force pushing down upon all sides of Senior and his stomach tightening and a snap of pain across his face and shooting to his neck and then no feeling and then only the dark, which brought with it a silence. Sterile, not peaceful. There was only the dark and this silence, as if in a small room, though still a consciousness within it. A thought – would there ever again be anything else? And a rising feeling from the center of such thought, like holding breath, rising and rising, and with it a pressure and a pain expanding.

And then the brightest of light and a rushing of air down into the void of the feeling.

Senior brought his head back from the air bag with great pain and an immediate stiffness in his neck running down to his back. There was some heavy material like dust swirling about and settling in the air of a light hue. Senior coughed dryly as he looked around the cab with his thoughts coming together. The windshield was gone. There was shattered glass everywhere. The telephone pole was only a few feet away from him as it had cut through the front of the truck deep into the engine compartment. Senior turned his neck with more pain to his side and then to the backseat, empty except for debris. Senior found the shotgun down on the floor of the passenger seat. He leaned as he could for it, but could not move more than a few inches with the seatbelt. Senior groped about for the release at his side. He found it and popped the belt free. Senior could not help but to moan from the pain as he leaned over and retrieved the gun. He sat back up and took several breaths. Pain was setting in all over, most deeply in his chest. Senior felt at the door for the handle. He pulled the handle and pushed the door open a half foot with it getting stuck. Senior bit down and leaned over and lined up the sole of his left boot and kicked the door and kicked again and again until it had swung open half-way through this impasse. Senior leaned up again and then stepped out of the truck, with both hands now taking hold of the shotgun.

There was glass and debris all around on the desert floor. Senior walked slowly forward and stepped sideways a few feet to create some short distance between him and the wreckage of the truck and a wider angle from which to view the land in front of the truck. The man's body was lying on the dirt some twenty yards in front of the truck, clear onto Senior's land, past the border fence. The man was face down, with his long black hair draped about. Senior watched him there. The man did not move. Senior walked forward until he reached the fence.

CHAPTER 6 – BOUND

Senior watched the man lying there on ground for some more moments from the fence. Senior reached over and dropped the gun on the ground on the other side of the fence. With pain pushing through most all of his body, Senior pulled down the top wire of the fence about a foot and held it down as he swung his left leg up and then over the wire, shifting his hips and weight then to face his chest down upon the top wire. With the weight of his torso now pushing down upon the wire, he slid his left foot down almost to the ground and shifted his weight that way and fell down to the dirt on that side of the fence. He rolled over in the pain, tightening all his body and staying there a moment. With closed eyes, he reached out his hand and took hold of the gun and pushed himself up to kneeling and then to standing. There was no giving in until it was done. Otherwise it would be her that would find this thing, and it finding her. And that upon his soul for all the rest of time.

Senior released the safety. He stepped quiet as he could as he approached the man's body. That feeling of walking up upon a wounded animal and remembering the lesson that such an animal will wait for such proximity. Senior reached the man and stood over the thing's body with the gun pointed at the back of his head. Senior's thought was to kick the thing in its side, but he then just as quickly concluded that idea dumb as hell. His next thought was to say something. But he only looked on.

He needed time. He squeezed the trigger – the burst, the kick, and the sight of the man's head absorbing the buck and caving inwards. The burnt propellant in the air.

Senior dropped the gun in the next instant and took a step forward and bent down and rolled the man onto his back. Senior shuffled to stand behind the man's head. He bent down and took hold of the man under each of his armpits and lifted this upper-half of the man's torso and began to drag him backwards across the dirt.

Senior looked over his shoulder and saw the barn forty yards out. Senior looked back down to the man and kept on dragging. The man's ankles were no longer cuffed together. The man's hands were free and hanging with cuffs around the wrists and the remaining chain from each dangling.

Senior did not look back again, but only drug the man at a slow pace while shuffling backwards towards the barn. Senior pivoted his approach a bit so as to arrive at what he envisioned behind him would be the side of the barn. He kept on.

At last the front of the barn appeared at Senior's side. He looked over his shoulder and altered his course closer to the barn and then continued to shuffle backwards until he found its rear corner and pulled the body around this corner to the rear of the barn. He dropped the body there and turned.

Senior breathed heavy, with some wheeze at the top of each breath. He put both hands upon his knees and bent over and in his own mind said to himself again the mantra his mother had taught him as a child to slow the breath. Senior stared all the while at the cellar door on the ground at the bottom of the rear wall of the barn. Senior stepped forward and unclasped the door, which was without lock, and lifted the heavy door and swung it over until it came falling down upon the ground with a clang. Senior stared down the stairs leading into the cellar, which after some short feet were swallowed by the dark.

"Shit," he said with the realization. "Ah, shit."

Senior looked over to the man lying there. The front of the man's face was all mashed and distorted still and there was no movement to him, though Senior did not wish to draw close to examine whether the tremble was there yet and whether it was rising.

Senior walked by the man and to the side of the barn. He was limping badly and there was no helping it. Senior walked past the barn and onto the path. His home stood there before him. The sight of it felt like something of a vision that a man far away may conjure up within himself to imagine himself home. Senior limped fast as he could up the path to the back door of the house.

Senior stood still a moment at the door before reaching to the knob. He let out a breath and then reached for it and turned the knob and pulled open the door and stepped in. He stood there and listened. All was quiet. He listened more. "Jean!" he hollered out. He listened again. "Jean!" The quiet remained, and with it, a relief.

Senior limped across the kitchen and down the hallway to his study. He went quickly to the desk and pulled a large drawer open with such force that it came out of the socket and fell to the ground, with pencils and other various instruments falling. Senior bent down and grabbed the flashlight. On his way standing back up there was a pop from his back which took his breath from him and challenged his balance until he reached out his hand and found the wall.

Senior stood there. "No," he said in a controlled tone. Senior turned and walked out of the study and down the hall and across the kitchen and through the door back out to the yard and limped quick as he could again down the path back to the barn.

The man's entire body was shaking gently. Senior rushed to get hold of him again and began dragging him to the open cellar door waiting for them. Senior turned himself sideways as he drug the thing down the wooden stairs into the dark. There was no time for the light yet, he would have to travel this very last stretch in the black. The man's body trembled within his hands.

They reached the bottom of the stairs. Senior heard the gravel floor beneath his boots and he pivoted and pointed his rear toward the other end of the cellar and continued to shuffle. It was dark as could be here. Senior saw nothing, but only heard the gravel breaking beneath each step, the friction of the thing's body in the drag, and labored breaths. He must be close. Senior took five more steps and dropped the body to the dirt.

Senior got the flashlight out from his pocket and clicked it on and turned around. The tall industrial metal locker stood forth from five feet away with its door open and waiting. The gray beam showed it empty. It was bigger than he remembered. Seven feet tall, four and-a-half feet or so wide.

Senior shifted the beam of the flashlight to the dirt at the side of the locker. There were the two piles of thick iron chains, neatly coiled like a pair of black vipers sleeping in the dark. Senior limped over to the first of these chains and bent down and picked it up. The locking clasp laid beside it. He picked those up too. Senior raised himself up to standing with some more care lest his back give out. Senior straightened out and limped back over to the body.

The flashlight showed the man shaking with some more intensity now. Senior hurried to his side and set the flashlight down upon the dirt with the beam pointing at the man's side. Senior lifted up the man's torso so that he was in a seated position. To feel the progress of the man's trembling was far worse. Senior began wrapping the chain around the man's torso, pulling each loop around the man's body tight as he could before beginning the next. After several such loops, Senior let the man fall to the ground. The chain cut so tight at the man's arms that the skin sunk inwards almost an inch. Senior picked the man's torso up again and began looping the remainder of the chain around the man in the same fashion until he was out of chain altogether. Senior locked the clasp in place and stepped back. The thick black chain was bundled firm as could be around the man's torso with many passes. There was no tighter way to bind this thing. There was none.

Senior grabbed the man with his fingertips gripping the links of chain around his torso and drug the body back to the locker and then stepped to the side and threw the top half of the man inside. Senior repositioned himself and took hold of the man's legs and pushed the other half of his body inside and to the back of the locker. The flashlight only partially lit the scene from its position several feet away. Senior sat back and stared at the man sitting bound in the locker, leaning back against its rear wall.

Senior took several breaths and then turned and crawled

the few feet over to the flashlight. He picked it up and turned back to the locker. The man's eyes were now open and looking at him. Senior screamed out and dove forward and grabbed the door. He pushed it shut with a bang and him pushing with all his weight up against it to hold it closed.

The thing inside let out an unearthly scream, of a deep and rising tone to a roar. Such sound reverberating in the box set Senior to be still.

The chains began to rattle and the weight of the thing shifted some, but not altogether much. Senior had only a moment and he knew it.

Senior scrambled across the ground to the second pile of chains. He found also the two thick, industrial padlocks laying beside it. Senior took hold of the heavy chain in one arm and with the other hand grabbed both of these padlocks. Senior rushed back to the locker and found the handle and its opening. Senior dropped the chain there and found its end and took it and threaded the opening of the handle. He got to his feet and walked around the locker until he had circumnavigated it entirely and then threaded the end of the chain through the handle again and pulled the chain tight. He walked around the locker again. He did this two more times with room to thread the chain through the handle and then wrapped the chain above the top of the handle. He circled the locker again three more times until he was just about out of chain at the point by the handle again. Senior took one heavy padlock and found a spot where two links of the chain met closely at the handle and clasped the padlock tightly through the links and squeezed it shut.

It had become quiet. The thing inside listening. Senior stepped back and studied his work. The chains wrapped around the locker tight and thick like a belt.

The man screamed again and began to struggle from inside. Senior held his breath and paced slowly backwards as the thing thrashed about violently inside the box, making a terrible blend of sound from the chains and feet of the thing crashing against all sides of the locker. Senior held the dim beam of the light upon the center of the locker and waited in anticipation to see if such binding would hold him.

It drew quiet. The echo of these crashes faded away in the dark of the room and the dust-filled air. Senior stopped his pacing backwards and stood still and listened.

There was the sound of some shifting weight and the dragging of chain upon the floor of the locker. Then came the sound of such chain scraping up the side of the locker. The eyes of the man appeared in the top slit on the face of the locker, looking at Senior in the quiet that had at once gripped the place.

Those eyes were small from this distance, though Senior felt even from here the power rising from behind them and reaching out.

Senior backed away again, holding the beam upon this spot and watching as he went. At last Senior stumbled upon the first of the stairs leading upward. He turned and hobbled up the stairs. Halfway up the staircase he thought he heard the man say something in a sharp whisper, though he could not understand it and did not wait for the thing to repeat itself.

The light and the air of the world brought a relief like

waking from a nightmare. Senior stepped to the side of the cellar door, picked it up from the earth, and pushed it over on its hinges until it fell shut with a clang. Senior took the second padlock from the pocket of his pants and clamped it shut on the handle of the door and stepped back.

Senior waited and stared down at the door and listened more. He heard nothing. He eventually heard the cicadas buzzing from just out on the mesa land. Senior turned and walked away.

Senior's limp only continued to deteriorate as he walked across the land back toward the wreckage. There was the thought that he could turn for the house and collapse upon the living room couch until she found him. He would not let such thought remain for but a moment and continued forward toward the truck.

The trailer had broken free from the hitch during the crash and laid on its side some fifteen yards away from the truck. The walls were caved in at various places from the way it landed and rolled across the earth. The rear door was hanging open. It was quiet. Senior knew what he would find.

The horse was broken in all places, laying on her belly, with her legs sprawled out in various contortions. Her nose was still fastened to the far wall of the trailer by the leather strap leading to its halter ring, keeping the horse's head suspended in the air and looking up as if in prayer. Senior stood at the door of the trailer and looked at her.

Senior stepped in and navigated the debris around his feet until he reached the far wall. He unlatched the hook upon her halter ring and guided her head as gently as he could to the floor of the trailer, which was actually its side wall. Her dark eye was open and wet and looking at him with nothing behind it.

Senior scooted to her side and with much pain bent down and put his rear upon the floor next to her. He then laid back and rested the back of his head upon her side. He stared up at the blank metal of the inside wall of the trailer, which acted now as its ceiling. Every bit of his body throbbed in a pulsing pain, as did his jaw, which did not rest in proper alignment as it relaxed. This pain faded as his vision narrowed and darkened, as if looking down a tunnel that was closing around him until all was dark. And then quiet.

Senior came to, in and out of short bits of consciousness, and heard voices and recognized himself being moved and people talking to him and about him. He fell back into the dark and the quiet and remained there.

CHAPTER 7 – PRISONERS

Jean stood beside the hospital bed. Senior laid there with the upper half of his body inclined most all the way up. The both of them looked on at the nurse standing before them. Senior's face was bruised all over, with swelling over his left eye, closing it a bit. There was a cut across his bottom lip that was a deep purple and swollen with a lump.

The nurse read to Senior and Jean from a chart in her hands. "You got three ribs with fractures. Two on the left, one on the right there. Others bruised. Says here you also got a pulmonary contusion, that's a bruise on the lung, left lung. There's bruising deep to and around your sternum. A partial fracture on the left clavicle. Trauma to the muscles up through the shoulders and to the neck." The nurse looked up to Senior. "Likely was a concussion." She looked to Jean and then to Senior and then back down to the chart.

"They were most concerned about the dehydration, which was severe. Doctor underlined the word." The nurse flipped the chart around as if they might wish to see such a thing. "Probably why you blacked out. Most probably why you wrecked."

Senior and Jean were quiet.

"You remember that?" the nurse asked.

"Hmm?"

"Crashing?"

Senior looked at her as if processing and running back the events within such thought. "Parts of it, I guess."

The nurse kept looking on as if he was expected to continue. "Darling. I bet it all just hurts like hell, don't it?"

Senior nodded as his stare fell to her side, still processing such thoughts. "Hmm" - Senior sounded down in his throat.

"You find what you were looking for out there?" the nurse asked.

"I did not."

The hospital room went quiet. Jean put her hand upon Senior's upper arm.

"It probably don't feel like it, but the good Lord's hand was upon you. You lucky. You very lucky," the nurse said.

"Yes ma'am."

"You're going to be laid up a couple days here. We'll do our best to keep you comfortable. The both of you."

"Thank you ma'am."

"Okay then," the nurse said as she stepped to a cubby at the bed's end and dropped the chart in, with the pen hanging from its top on a chain rattling to still in the cubby. The nurse smiled and then left out.

Jean gently rubbed the middle of Senior's arm with her hand, looking down upon his face. Senior looked down at a spot on the blanket covering his lap.

"I'm real sorry," he said.

"My Lord. You got nothing to be apologizing about."

"I won't forget the sight of her."

Jean was quiet. Her face only sympathetic.

"You were first to find me?" he asked.

"I was."

"You saw her?"

"I only saw you."

Senior shook his head. "Damned waste. Damn it all."

"You could've died Samuel."

Senior only shook his head more, looking still at his lap.

"I don't give a damn about some horse," she said.

Senior looked to her, the whites of his eyes cracked red against a pink hue. Jean reached with her other hand to his forehead and placed her palm upon it. She ran her hand over his thick and matted hair of a deep gray. "What happened out there?" she asked.

Senior looked again to his lap. Jean ran her hand slowly over his hair again.

"Is our boy coming?" he asked.

"Beau's on his way now. He was down south county when I called. Picking up Susie on his way."

Senior nodded. "Good. That's good."

Jean kept to looking him over.

"When they run you out of here tonight, I don't want you going home," Senior said.

This brought something of a concern upon her face as she continued her calculating.

"You go and sleep at their house. You let them take care of you."

"I don't need anybody taking care of me Samuel."

Senior looked back to her. "Please do that for me."

Jean was quiet. She ran her hand gently across his scalp again. Senior's eyes fell back to his lap.

"Okay," she said. "Okay."

In a dream in the night, Senior saw the man standing at the foot of his hospital bed and staring down upon him. The thing's face was broken and caved inwards, like it had been when Senior had shot him point blank down under the mesa. The face was shaking and a rage was rising and rising as the man stood there, though he did not move. Waiting. When Senior awoke, he sat and listened to the quiet of the room and took in all the pain about every part of his body and prayed and thought about the dark of the place that he had put the man and what the thing was saying there and what he would do.

It was another two days before Senior could stand. And another before he could walk. And then two more before they let him go. Senior's arm on the side of the fractured clavicle was in a sling, with the other arm devoted to a cane to keep him upright, though walking was discouraged for more than but short distances for the week. Beau drove them all home to the ranch in his truck. They picked up supper on the way.

Senior was quiet throughout the meal, though he smiled at all that was said. Mostly Susie and Jean talked back and forth regarding the various happenings about town and the church in regards to Senior's event. Beau updated Senior some about the station over the last couple days and everyone's continued wishes for him. Senior only smiled, that presence of pain clinging somewhere beneath.

Senior insisted upon walking Beau and Susie out when it was time, over the protests of all, which he would not have. Upon Beau saying his goodbye, Senior stepped in close to him and set the cane against the open door and wrapped his free arm around Beau and brought him in close and hugged him. Senior held him there for several moments, just held him. When Senior released Beau a bit, he brought his hand to the side of Beau's face and held it there and brought Beau in and kissed him upon his forehead. The faces of all, including Beau, were of some profound emotion moving and of surprise and of recognition. Senior brought his head back and patted Beau's face twice and looked into his eyes. Senior grabbed for the cane at his side, got hold, turned, and limped down the hallway, leaving the three there at the doorway staring at each other with each their expressions still intact. Senior disappeared into the living room.

Jean built a fire and retrieved the book that Senior had been reading at night before all this had happened and gave it to him.

"You remember where you were?" she asked.

Senior flipped through the book. He shook his head. "I'm starting all over."

They read beside the fire, with it providing the only light and the only noise in the living room. After about an hour of this, Jean closed her book.

"Let's get on up to bed then Samuel."

Senior kept his book open. "You go on."

"I will not. There's no discussion to it. I'm putting you to bed."

Senior dropped the book to his lap and looked down at it for a moment. He looked to Jean. "I'm restless. In my skin." He shook his hands out. "I just need a bit."

What was at first a stern look upon Jean's face of some conviction on the matter began to soften in the moment until it was gentle in her thought. "You're not going up those stairs by yourself. You just aren't. When you're ready, you holler."

Senior nodded.

"I'm so very glad you're home." Jean began walking out of the room and looked back at Senior just as she was leaving.

"You're everything," he said.

Her footsteps in the hall stopped.

"All of it," Senior said louder.

It was quiet. Her footsteps began again down the hall and then up each of the stairs.

Senior sat and watched the fire slowly die out over the next hour until there were but soft specks of embers glowing in the pile. Until he was in the dark. The house was quiet. He had not heard her above for a half-hour. Senior sat there fifteen minutes longer, listening to the quiet.

Senior pushed himself up to standing. He leaned on the cane as he stepped quietly as he could across the living room and to the hall and then down to his study. There on his desk were the various items he had on his person when they had found him. His keys were there. The flashlight was there. He took both of these in his hand and walked out of the study. Senior walked back down the hallway to a coat closet. He opened the door and found there a light cotton pullover. He put this on and found places for the keys and flashlight in its pockets and zipped it up. Senior walked back down the hall to the living room and then to the kitchen and to the back door. His boots were by the door. Senior scooted out a kitchen chair and pulled the boots to its bottom. He cringed as he sat down upon the chair. His ankles were yet very stiff. Those joints creaked as if made of a worn plywood as he forced his boots upon his feet. Senior leaned heavy on the edge of the table and stood up.

Senior stepped to the backdoor and unlocked it. He listened again. He looked back to the entry of the kitchen, with the living room out past it as he listened more. There was nothing to hear. Senior turned that old knob and pulled the door ajar softly and then opened it all the way. He opened also the screen door in this quiet fashion and closed the both of them as he stepped out.

The barn out on the land stood forth only as a black form, with no definition or contrast within its outlines. The cloud cover scattered about was blocking out the moon and stars above. It was a very dark night out on that desert world beyond. Senior turned on the flashlight and pointed it down the porch steps. With one arm in the sling, he would have to choose between the light and the cane, and he chose the light. He set out in his limp down each of the stairs slow and then hobbling down the path towards the barn.

A family of coyotes out distant on the plain yelped frantic, rounding up their victim. Or victims. The crickets chimed back and forth. Senior's steps crackled upon the broken gravel, drawing near to the dark form of the barn.

Senior stood just by the cellar door and listened for any noise from the thing below. It was absolute quiet down there. Senior listened two minutes longer. He turned the padlock loose with the key and removed the lock and set it upon the ground. He lifted the cellar door up and swung it open with a creak coming from its hinges and set it down upon the ground. The air which rushed out from the dark was hot even amongst the temperature of the summer night's air.

Senior pointed the flashlight down the staircase. He thought he heard the rattle of chains, but he was not certain. Senior limped slowly as he could down the stairs, step by step, each loud within this place.

The sound certain of chains moving came forth from the dark.

When Senior reached the bottom of the stairs, he stood still and pointed the flashlight out at the locker far on the other side of the cellar. He allowed a deep breath in, which brought with it an equal measure of pain up into his ribcage and chest. Senior limped forward.

Ten feet out, the eyes could be seen through the top slit. The man was quiet. Senior stopped only three feet from the locker door, looking straight into the black centers of those eyes, surrounded by a sharp cream color without imperfection. These eyes did not communicate a rage as Senior had expected. They were almost gentle, though Senior had readied his mind for a deception.

"You all right?" the man asked in his deep voice, now with a rasp to it.

"I'm alive."

"You get what you wanted?"

"I wouldn't put it like that."

They looked at one another. The man's eyes scanned down Senior's broken body. "What is this place?" the man asked.

"It's where you are. And where you will be so long as I'm alive."

"You think it will keep me?"

"You're still here."

"Maybe I was waiting to see you again."

"Get on with it then."

The man just stared back at Senior. Whatever soft tone that was in those eyes faded away somewhere out into the dark around them.

"I guess it was you I had this place ready for," Senior said.

The man stayed quiet.

"You recall that man I was telling you about when we were out on the highway?"

"The murderer."

"Judge found a problem with the story leading to the warrant they used to get into that trailer of his. Threw the evidence out and the case with it. Order showed up on my desk to let him go."

The thing looked on.

"I walked the man out the facility to the street myself and put him in a cab to a hotel just outside the county, where he had a one-night stay paid for, like any other man held for that amount of time if they so chose. Mind you, this guy had never showed even the beginning of an emotion. Ever. As the cab left out, this devil, he smiled at me."

Senior drew quiet, picturing it all in his head.

"I stood there five minutes thinking about that. I went to my office and thought on it a half-hour longer. Son of a bitch smiled at me."

Senior shook his head as if he was in that office. "I set all this up that afternoon. Drove out to the hotel that night. Broke into his room as he was sleeping and snatched him. Brought him back here and locked him up. I kept him down here in this dark six weeks. By then, he was just crying all the time. Pissin' and shittin' on himself and whimpering out at me."

It drew quiet again. Senior not looking at the man's eyes, but down a half-foot and thinking. "I took him out a two-hour drive to the middle of the desert down south. Made him strip off all his clothes. So that he was like a naked, shaking babe on the dirt there. And I took my shotgun, double-barrel, and I pointed it at that face of his and held it there thirty seconds with him cringing up pathetic."

The man's eyes were unchanged.

"And then I pulled the gun back. Walked back to my truck. And left him there. I saw him standing through the rearview and calling out for me as if he then wished I would come back and shoot him. I didn't look back again."

"You didn't kill him?"

"Left that to the Lord."

"You going to let me out then?"

"I'm not ever coming back down here."

The thing's eyes were still unmoved.

"You take the years you got here and find the fear of Him," Senior said. It was a long moment. "I come down just to let you know what you were in for. You won't see me again."

Senior backed away and then turned and began walking.

"You all are just like me," the man said, stopping Senior. "Before our time together is up, I'm going to teach you about that. That's a lesson that's going to hurt in its learning."

Senior stood there. He did not turn back, but said,

"Better keep you locked up then. Until the judgment."

Senior limped slow to the stairs in the quiet and then up them and then out of that place.

CHAPTER 8 – THE QUIET SETTLING IN

Jean woke Senior a half-hour before the sun was up and reminded him that she had to be to service early as it was her rotation in the choir. Senior said he still wished to go. Senior was quiet on the drive over to the church, staring as he was out his window at that empty and sprawling desert wilderness, the pale sun at the beginnings of again stretching out its authority across it. Jean left him quiet, but looked at him often, and talked to the Lord within herself.

Senior did not go into the sanctuary with Jean. He sat in the car out in the parking lot alone. He was not settled that what it was he would carry into that place was all the way right or true. Even if his conclusion was that the sum of it was. The Almighty would see. Senior did not yet wish to cross the threshold. Though as he looked out on that world expanding without end, he reminded himself that there were no thresholds, that all the world was yet a footstool.

Senior caught movement a half-mile out on a ridge on the mesa land, and then more movement of a figure there. Senior found himself opening the car door and getting himself out and to standing. He limped as he could out to the very edge where the parking lot met the dirt beginnings expanding out to the open space.

Senior squinted his eyes at the ridge, focusing as he could upon it. He at last made out a mountain lion that had stopped in its stride, looking in his direction, as if it had seen him even at this great distance, and had been told by that voice which guides it through that world to stop and look at the man. It was just staring at him. It sat its rear down upon the ground.

Senior could not remember the last time he had seen one wild. The distance between them removed the reality of its presence like those older stories and myths of the desert lands themselves which exist only far away, though their truths cannot be denied in some place connected, even if they cannot be touched, or themselves touch the onlooker. Senior stared at it, and it back at him, thirty seconds and quiet.

The lion got up quick as if snapped back to attention and set out on a jog over the ridge and disappeared. Senior stayed looking at that spot. He walked out another twenty feet upon the dirt and stood and looked more. He then leaned on the cane in setting himself down to sitting on the ground. He stayed there. Even as he heard people parking their cars and talking and going into the church somewhere behind, he stayed. Surveying the stage. Until it was an absolute quiet again.

He looked out over the mesa lands running to hills out distant on the horizon. A pair of cicadas began a gentle hum from somewhere out in the brush to his side. The early morning sun was soft upon it all. He brought his bent knees together as he was sitting there on the dirt and folded his hands atop them. There came welling up from his chest a feeling like wanting to cry. It accumulated and rose to his throat and he clinched it and bit down his jaw tight to keep it in. He did not know who he would be crying for, or what it was that drew it from him. He tried to clear his throat and coughed and a tear came from the corner of his eye and ran down the worn and bruised skin atop his cheek before he could wipe it away.

He recalled there the last time such feeling had overcome him, on the day they buried his oldest boy in the earth out back of the church those many years ago. Down in that sad and simple plot by itself on the edge of those grounds. He cleared his throat again.

The cicadas at once drew quiet together. And it was quiet all around him.

PART II – BEAU

TWO YEARS LATER

CHAPTER 9 – BURIED

- Beau

Dad would take my older brother Sam and I out into the country when we were boys. In the cold seasons we would hunt the antelope that roamed across the mesa lands, carrying their corpses home on the backs of our horses like wild men. When it was warmer, we would spend the days drifting. We wandered the canyons and climbed the mesa heads, scouring the open space as kings of that untamed land.

Dad would let us drink coffee as we rode out after him into the cold and dark of those mornings. I see his silhouette, swaying atop his horse, the rising sun filling that morning horizon with pink and purple and golden streaks. He looks out over that ancient face of New Mexico, her bare hills growing to mountain peaks in the distance, the layered rock face of the canyons speaking of her epochs, old as time itself.

Sam (Junior was what everyone else called him) woke me in the middle of the night late one fall. Dad had been called up north somewhere. There had been a bad accident on the highway, some people had died. Sam wanted to set out into the country on our own. It was wrong. I knew it was wrong. I pretended to be asleep, but Sam wouldn't have it. He got me as far as loading my horse up alongside his and riding out to the gate, but I could go no further and stopped. He turned back his horse and looked at me for a long moment with disappointment across his face. He shrugged his shoulders and neck as if shrugging some weight off of himself before turning his horse back around to the road and setting out. I've often wondered what I looked like in that moment. What he saw.

Sam was not back when I awoke a couple hours later that morning. He was not back when Dad returned sometime around noon. He was not back when the sun had set on the day. Momma was going crazy. Just crazy. I knew then as I know now that I would never see him again. That next day, Momma and Dad told me that he had fallen off his horse somewhere out in the country and had hit his head. When Momma left the room crying, Dad went on to tell me that Sam had come to rest from the fall in something like a puddle no more than six inches deep and that he had drowned. Drowned. In the middle of that desert. And he was gone.

I would have saved him from that. Without much effort at all. He would not have died choking in an inconsequential bowl of mud on the ground. He would not be in a box, this very moment. I knew that then. I know that now. I'm sure Dad did too, though he never said a word to this effect, even when I said it about myself. I can't say that I know in specific terms how that conclusion has shaped me. The life I've lived from then until now. The way I see the world. Though I can tell you that I carry it. It'll be mine to carry until the grave, maybe after.

The strong are not strong at all. God's plan is a

narrative which displaces such with the ease of an author's pen – while leaving those alongside to think about their own choices in the matter. It's plain to me, as it should be to you. Both the pen and the choice ought to be feared. For against the pen there is no man that could stand. And the choice. The choice tells of who you are. And what man could stand against the truth of himself. All he can do is mourn it. Run from it he cannot.

The calf stared up into the heavens with the glazed, empty eyes of the dead. Its tongue stuck to the desert floor amidst a dried pool of blackened blood. The front of its throat was crushed over the top of its trachea, but was not punctured in the slightest. The meat from both of its hindquarters had been stripped, leaving its femurs cleaned to a bleached pearl. The rest of its body told nothing of the struggle, or even of the distance that the poor thing had been drug across the plain. Unabused. Seemingly untouched.

The rest of the herd was staring on from about fifty yards off, except the calf's momma, who was looking over Beau's shoulder as he knelt down beside her young one. She snorted and carried on with a sort of shuffle of her feet, looking at the calf, as if he might somehow put the pieces of her back together. Beau stood up and patted her behind her ears. He looked into her eyes for a moment as if to say something. But he did not.

"You taking a look Pop?" Beau asked as he walked back towards the rest of the group, putting his gloves on.

Senior did not reply. He stared off north toward the beginnings of canyon country, never having dropped off his horse. A chilled breeze swept across the desert plains.

Blankets of clouds carrying the makings of a snowstorm gathered over the mountain peaks out past the canyons.

Ed and his oldest Ed Jr., all of about sixteen, were also on horses beside Senior. "You're not going to take a look Sheriff?"

"I don't believe I will Ed." Senior spat a stream of tobacco out past the other side of his horse, scanning his gaze back over the plain to where the calf lay. "If it's all the same to you."

Beau made it back to his horse and pulled his rifle out of its holster beneath the satchel. He dug back down deep in the satchel and removed a pouch. He took a handful of rounds from the pouch and chambered each of them.

Senior smiled and spat again down beside his horse. "Don't know what in the hell you're doing that for."

"You don't think you'll find it?" Ed hollered again.

Senior scanned the plain again back toward the canyons. "Make sure any more of the little ones you got make it all the way home."

Beau and Senior rode straight north across the plains toward Maes canyon. Beau had been able to make out its trail for the first mile or so as they rode along, but lost it at a rough turn of beargrass and cacti. Senior kept on without needing to take a second look. The breeze pushing out from the canyons had stiffened to a wind and had grown bitter. Flurries began to appear here and there in the ever darkening air. They rode slowly, bundled within thick wool blankets pulled tightly around them. Beau had tilted his cowboy hat down over his brow to shield his face and kept a lowered gaze similar to that of his horse. Senior kept his gaze high despite it all, as if such a cold could no longer penetrate the callus that had grown over the years upon his face. The scar running from underneath his grayed mustache down his cheek had turned a crimson with the cold.

They set up a small camp a mile out from the beginning of the canyons. Senior wouldn't hear of bringing the horses along any further, said he had to put one of Momma's horses down many years ago out in those parts on account of it breaking a leg. He said he could not do that again. Would not do that again. Said she would smell them anyways. They tethered them at the camp and set out.

They took position on a flattened rock the size of a mattress which overlooked the gorge below. They laid out on their stomachs with their heads coming to the end of the rock, blankets atop their backs, rifles cradled underneath with the barrels hanging out just to the edge of the rock itself. The moon was full behind the cloud cover above in the center of the night sky, pouring its gray light through the milky bodies to the world below with scattered effectiveness. At times, the floor of the gorge some one-hundred feet below was alight with this quiet gray. Moments later, the clouds would shift and the entire gorge would become darkness itself.

There was a black pool of water down on the low point of the gorge where the rain and snowmelt gathered. There were not many such pools around this side of the canyons. Senior walked over to another point along the edge of the gorge and dropped the open vial of urine so that it would fall and smatter on a pile of brush and debris that had gathered near the pool below. Without a moment's notice, the entire floor of the gorge would be as dark as the grave and not even Senior would descend to perform this task. "Piss falls the same from here," he whispered.

They laid out on that rock watching the floor of the gorge for some time. The winds had altogether ceased about an hour in. A silence and still had taken hold of the night. Gray streaks of light continued to break through the cloud cover every couple of minutes to illuminate the gorge and its empty floor below, only to be swallowed up again and again by a black that the night poured into the gorge until it overflowed. The monotony of this steady rhythm soon drowned all suspense like a great pocket watch waving ever before their eyes.

After two hours Senior had fallen asleep with his chin resting on folded hands that had been propping his face up over the butt of his rifle. Beau continued to stare down into the gorge with heavy eyes – the gray would fill the gorge quietly to reveal the same empty picture as before, and then again the darkness would pour on in to cover everything. Over and over he watched this cycle unfold and fold up again upon itself. Beau found himself thinking about the calf's momma. Her eyes filled with such a pain, such a helplessness, such a searing regret toward the knowledge that the things which are cannot be undone. Beau had seen such things in the eyes of people. The very same. He thought about that. He pondered if that breath which fills our eyes really is the very breath which fills the eyes of all those that crawl about our world, as the Book says. God's breath. That as God's judgment fell heavy upon Adam and his seed, so too it fell upon all such as these which share our breath. That the calf's momma wasn't cursing some beast so much as she cursed Adam and all the death that has grown from his bones. That the calf's momma was bemoaning Adam's representative right there leaning over the carcass of her only lot in this cursed stage, where she was caught up between his sin and consequence.

The gorge had been sitting beneath the dark phase of this cycle for several minutes. As the moonlight was again allowed to creep into the gorge, Beau saw her – the grayed outline of a large mountain lion pawing and sniffing about the brush beside the pool below. The sight of her did not register for several seconds. When it did, a chill shot across Beau's chest, causing his lungs to restrict and suck in the cold of the night air with an awkwardness. It was not altogether much louder than an ordinary breath, but she heard. The lion did an about-face and looked up directly at Beau. Although her body remained a hueless gray, the almond of her eyes was set aflame with the moonlight as her gaze focused upon him. For a moment she simply stared up at him without any emotion upon her face. Suspicious, if not afraid. Beau wondered if she was able to see him at all as he could not have appeared more clearly than a dark outline with the moonlight pouring in from above and behind him in the sky.

The lion's eyes thinned with a reserved ferocity. She opened her mouth, showing a set of long teeth that glowed a brilliant white. Beau's thought centered all in a moment. He took hold and pointed his rifle down at her. Senior's hand appeared and wrapped itself over the top of the rifle where Beau's hands gripped.

"Son." Senior's face was tight and grave. The sides of his mouth crooked downward as if he were weathering some terrible taste.

Senior removed his hand from Beau's rifle and placed it upon his own. Senior himself took aim. The lion dropped to something of a crouch in an instant and began leaning to its left – the crack of the rifle shook the ground around them. The impact of the round made a deep thudding sound of a heavy bluntness just before the echo of the rifle shot bounced back off of the gorge floor and reverberated off its walls. The lion was pushed into a violent spin and twist, hitting the floor first on its head and shoulders. The lion gave three jerks on the ground before it pushed out a wild scream. The lion continued to jerk several times, even rolling over before its body fell still. The echoes of the blast and the scream faded into the breadth of the world around them.

A quiet set in. The lion's face and body were covered in shadow, showing only her outline.

The lion let out another cry. The cry was much deeper. Filled with a labored desperation. Its body had not moved. Beau heard Senior clear the round. The rifle again exploded. A ring shot through Beau's ear and filled his mind with a pain. He did not hear the impact this time, but saw the lion's body absorb the round, do a half spin on the ground and roll over. The lion came to rest being bent up against the gorge wall in an unnatural contortion, with its lower half folded beneath the top half of its body.

Beau felt a tightness in his jaw. As the moments passed, he realized that his bite was set in a clinch. The sharpness to the ring in his head shifted to a lower tone and began to throb. Senior brought his head out from its tucked position behind the rifle. He stared down at her. His eyes visibly moist.

Senior would not let Beau touch her. Like she was something of a sickness that he could not be exposed to. He gritted his teeth as he dragged her by her hind legs across the canyon floor. He lifted her legs to his waist and then shuffled backwards for several steps before releasing his breath and letting her weight fall to the ground, attempting to catch his breath for a few moments before he began again. He was always looking away from her. After fifteen minutes of this, Senior could no longer budge her more than a couple feet at a time, though he tried.

"Can't be done," Beau said.

Senior breathed heavily. He fell down to one knee and looked off onto a spot on the ground. "Yeah, well. I ain't leaving her for the crows." He continued to look on that spot. "Nope."

Senior rose to his feet and looked to Beau, still in some train of thought. "Okay then." Senior turned and began to walk back out the way they had come down.

"What you want to do?" Beau asked.

Senior continued walking, clutching his hips with his hands and arching his back with soreness. "Get me that shovel of yours."

Beau sat down and leaned up against the wall of the canyon. He pulled a can of tobacco from his pocket, took a thick pinch, and packed it beneath his lip. His breathing seemed loud amidst the quiet in the canyon, beside the still of her body. Still, but nothing of peaceful. Even now she lay so unnaturally. A beautiful thing made crooked. Artificially so. Altogether unlike the calf of the morning for whom he no longer felt anything of pity. He did not touch her and dared not look in her eyes.

Senior returned carrying the abbreviated camping shovel, a can of lighter fluid, and his wool blanket. Senior dug a wide and shallow hole in the caliche, piling the dirt and sediment at its side. Senior laid her on her side in the hole. He shrouded her with the brush and debris blown and gathered in the corner nearby. He poured the entirety of the lighter fluid on her body up to her neck. He wrapped a white rag around her face. They watched her burn.

When the smell became too much, Beau stepped back. Senior stepped forward, breathing all the same. When the flames had died out, Senior laid his own blanket atop her body and shoveled the dirt back over her. The fire had burned much of her coat and skin, but did not consume her. Her grave was not deep. They set four large rocks over it to keep anything from digging at her.

They did not talk during the walk back to the horses. They packed up quietly too. When they got atop the horses, Beau started out. After several moments he saw that Senior had not followed. Beau trotted his horse back to him. Senior stared out at a full moon beginning to fall closer to the horizon in the west. Beau had not noticed that the clouds had moved on south, leaving the moon naked in the lightening sky.

"Some things cannot just be buried away," Senior said. "You understand?"

"I don't think fires much help with things of that kind either."

Senior pulled a can of tobacco from his pocket and packed his lower lip. He cleared his throat deeply and spat. "A fool goes on looking for things he doesn't want to find."

"She was taking folks' cattle."

76

Senior kept on looking out at that moon.

"Am I missing something?" Beau asked again. "You had to."

Senior thought about that. "Be careful about the things you have to do. 'For long, they pile on up and that's all you are." Senior started as if he was going on to say something else, but then he stopped. "Shit son. I'm sorry about all this."

CHAPTER 10 – GONE

- Beau

My momma cannot be lied to. It can't be done. Not by me and I suspect not by anyone. I haven't seen it. She has a gift, from God she says, to pick out a lie no matter how it gets buried or dressed up by the schemes of men.

I might have been thirteen or fourteen the last time I tried. I can't for the life of me remember the lie itself, though I know that Momma had let me draw it out for some time. She sat me down at the kitchen table with her Bible laid right out on the place setting. She didn't open it, but spoke as if she were reading gospel. She said I first needed to understand that the Book says there wasn't ever a lie that was an orphan, no matter how small it was, as all such things have but only one father in the evil one himself. That though we all were created in the image of father God, that those who lie don't want to bear such image, but rather some fabricated skin of their own liking. That such wrap themselves in this skin and create false worlds, where they sit as false kings for such a time until the lie becomes a reality entire, while all the time the truth cinches tighter and tighter around their necks back here in the real world until there ain't nothing that can be done to deny the pain. But by then of course, there ain't nothing can be done at all.

She said, don't lie to me. She said, don't lie to yourself. She said, son, you can't lie to God. There ain't no world but this one. And there ain't no noose but His own.

Beau and Senior rode along the same path that they had come. A pink sun crawled over the horizon of the mesas out east, painting the landscape in a quiet purple that would fade and fade as the sun ascended until there was nothing poetic about the barren earth around them in the plain light of the morning. They made it back to Ed's ranch around nine. Ed's wife Debbie saw them riding up from the kitchen window and came out to the porch. "Ed and Junior are still about watering the horses."

"That's okay Deb. I'll ring him this afternoon," Senior said.

"No, no, no. I've spent the better part of the last hour and a half setting up a spread for the both of you."

"Oh, yeah?"

"Eggs, hash browns, grits, cakes – not less than three plates of bacon. Couldn't ask for nothing more."

"Can I count on you not to go and tell Jean about said bacon?" Senior asked.

"Who is it that you think you're talking to?"

"Serious as the grave."

"Well I'll take it to my grave. 'Long with the rest of my trunk of secrets."

Senior and Beau ate from full plates before them as Debbie sat on the other side of the table chatting them up with no plate of her own. They talked about church. About Beau and Susie's plans for babies, and how many. About Ben Moore's funeral and how nice it was how many people showed up. About remembering Ben's brother Hunter, and how not half as many came to his service a couple years back. About how money was tight for everyone and how strange it was that a couple hundred dollars a month could change a person's life so. About people out in California who could not imagine such things.

Ed and Ed Jr. came through the door as Senior and Beau were finishing their second plates. "Morning Sheriff. Beau," Ed called as he removed his hat and placed it on a hanger by the door.

Senior nodded as he chewed a full mouth of food.

"Been out all night. Guess you were right then," Ed began.

"About what?" Senior answered while swallowing the end of that mouthful.

"Well you didn't find him, did you?"

Senior paused for a moment looking down at his plate, as if he were making some split second decision. He loaded another fork-full of eggs. "Her."

"What's that?"

"The lion was a female. Her."

"She was still plenty big," Beau interjected.

"I can't say as that I'm surprised. Besides Deb here, females have always been something crosswise towards me."

"She is a thorn no longer," Senior said, biting his biscuit.

"You exterminated her?"

"Exterminated?"

"Exterminated. Yeah. You know, dispatched. Eradicated. Killed, shit."

Senior chewed his biscuit and thought about such descriptions. He shook his head with a chuckle. "She is deceased. Very much so."

"What'd you do with her? I didn't see her outside."

"I didn't suspect that you would've."

Ed stared back at Senior with a bewildered smile.

"We didn't bring her."

"Didn't bring her? Where the hell is she?"

"Nowhere."

"Nowhere?"

Senior sipped coffee from a mug and confirmed his answer with a nod. Ed looked to Beau to see if Beau would reveal anything further. Beau stared back politely.

"Now Sheriff, she was your prize of course, and you know I ain't the kind of fella that would slink his way into what's yours, but, if you don't have it in mind to take her... I'd like to have her."

Senior sucked some remaining biscuit out from in between his teeth with a smack, sizing Ed's intentions.

"Ellis is a whiz with hides. He could make out as good a spread as could be made. I don't doubt if we could get a grand out of such a thing."

Senior looked down to his plate with something like a smile on his face, lines of anger crept out its sides. "Yep." He set the coffee mug down, scooted his chair back, and rose from the table. He took his cowboy hat from the table and fixed it upon his head. Beau took the cue and rose as well. Senior looked to Debbie. "I'm going to hold you to that promise of yours."

Debbie seemed to realize that an awkwardness had sprung in the situation. She smiled and nodded.

Senior walked to the door, followed closely by Beau. Beau threw a look to Debbie as he passed as if he himself did not understand what had happened. Senior tipped his hat as he passed close by Ed, but did not make eye contact with him. As Senior walked out the front door, Beau stopped short next to Ed. He began to try to say something, but could not figure it. Beau raised his hand. Ed shook it, with a look of confusion that had begun to give way to a feeling of insult. Beau walked out the front door.

No one came out of the house as Senior and Beau loaded their horses in the trailer. Beau fixed the hitch of the trailer to the back of a raised dual-cab truck that bore black and gold paint with large SHERIFF decals across its sides. Beau saw that Debbie watched them from out the kitchen window as they drove off down the ranch road. When they got to the end of Ed's road, Beau hopped out and opened the gate for Senior to drive the truck and trailer through. An old turkey vulture was perched up on the telephone wire above, looking down the highway and waiting for something to die. Beau got back into the truck. They turned left onto Highway 19 and started for home some twenty-five miles north and east.

Highway 19 is an old two-laner in ill repair. Beau attempted to rest his head against the passenger-side window to nod off, but could not get more than ten seconds of peace before the truck was jolted by a pothole or some other defect. He kept on leaning against it all the same. Senior drove in quiet for several minutes.

"How much do you know about Uncle Winston?" Senior asked, breaking the quiet.

Beau opened his eyes and looked at Senior with a tired glare as if to say that he would have preferred the quiet. Beau shut his eyes again and rested his head back against the glass. "All right. What about Winston?"

"What do you know of him?"

"This is granddad's brother, right?"

"Baby brother."

"Well. I never met the man. I think I remember you mentioning something about him being a card player or something."

"He was a con. Conman. Got himself shot out back of some bar in Nevada over some money."

Beau opened his eyes and tilted his head to see Senior go on.

"Granddad took me with him to drive up there to see Winston in the hospital. They told Granddad he was dying. I was all of about thirteen or so. Hadn't seen Winston more than a handful of times that I could remember. I'll tell you, I've never forgotten his face since. It was like an, an off green-like color, you know? His eyes yellowish, on account of the kidneys failing. Like a dead man. They had broken a part of his jaw before they shot him. Doctors knew he was dying, so they didn't even bother to go about wiring it. He would try to sputter something out here and there to Granddad, but it was like some kind of torture to do so. Granddad didn't say much to him. Just sat there holding his hand and looking at him. We sat there for a day and a half in that room. Winston kept on declining all the time. About an hour before he passed, Granddad got me out of the hall and told me that Winston wanted to tell me something. I went on in, sat down. He looked into my eyes like I have never before or since seen. Looked down to some deep part of me. To grab hold of that part for what he was intending to say…"

Beau saw that Senior had spotted something out on the road ahead. Senior pumped the brakes. Beau looked back to the road, a car was pulled over on the opposite side of the highway, facing the direction from which they had come. The rear driver-side tire had blown out entirely. An older Hispanic cowboy, perhaps in his sixties, dressed in jeans and a plaid shirt and hat, was sitting on top of the trunk looking at them rolling by. Senior pulled the truck over to the shoulder on their side of the highway until it came to a stop. Senior shook his head as he looked out at the man on the car. "That's about the sum of it all, ain't it?" Senior put the truck in park. "I guess we better help this old boy out." He tilted the rear view mirror down to take an inventory of his appearance.

"What did he say to you?" Beau asked.

"What?"

"Winston. What did he say?"

"He said, 'A man is what he does. The rest is bullshit.' Said there was no such thing as sorry."

Senior and Beau got out of the truck and crossed over the highway to the car. It was a white, four-door Honda Civic of a couple years old with temporary plates from a dealership. The old man remained seated on top of the trunk with his boots resting on the bumper. He smiled politely.

"That's a shame," Beau said as him and Senior reached the car.

"Sir?" the man replied.

"Just bought her and she's already bitchin' at you."

The man laughed sharply, looking to the ground and rubbing his forehead. "Oh, yeah. Well, I wouldn't blame her. There was some kind of scrap wood, I guess, back there. It made a hell of a noise. Must've had some nails still in it."

"Usually folks around here would pick up something like that," Senior said. "Where you coming from?"

"Albuquerque."

"They didn't sell you a spare up there?"

"Guess not. You know, didn't think to even ask. It's all right though, my buddy is on his way. We'll get it all sorted out."

"Where's he coming from?" Senior asked.

"Silver. He shouldn't be long."

"He bringing a tow?"

"A tow? No. He was bringing one of those, what do you call em'... like the small tires?"

"A donut?" Beau interjected.

"Yeah, yeah. There's no need for you all to bother."

"Least we could do is get it jacked up for you so that you can be on your way all the quicker," Senior said. "I don't imagine they off and stiffed you on the jack too."

"I feel a damn fool about the whole thing, but you know, just didn't come to mind to check. It's used you know."

"We haven't even got your name."

"Nicolas."

"Well, Nicolas, I got my jack back there in the truck. I'll tell you what, I'll go on and get it. You hop off the trunk there and I'll be right back."

"He won't be but a few minutes."

"I'm insisting. It's the least we could do." Senior checked the highway in both directions and started walking back to the truck on the other side. "On second thought, son, you want to come on back and help me move some

85

things around to get to my tools?"

Beau followed Senior across over the blacktop. Senior was walking sideways-like, with his head turned to be able to look over Beau's shoulder. The man remained seated on the trunk of the car, but had turned his upper body so that he could look down the highway to the south from where Senior and Beau had come to be able to see oncoming cars.

Senior walked around to the other side of his truck to the rear passenger-side door and opened it. Beau came up alongside. Senior was not moving to get into the truck. He was watching the man through the cab window. The man was still looking down the highway.

"What are you doing? Everything's in the toolbox in the bed."

Senior continued to stare at the man. "Look at that. Still hasn't jumped down."

Beau looked at the man. "So?"

"Thinking we got ourselves a runner here."

Beau looked again. "Are you looking at this guy? What is he, seventy?"

"You got your sidearm?"

"It's up front."

"Put it on."

"Shit. You're serious."

Senior looked to Beau with every bit of serious upon his brow.

"All right." Beau opened the front passenger-side door and retrieved his sidearm holster with the glock locked in. He clipped it to the belt over his jeans at his hip. "I didn't see a piece."

Senior was still staring at the man through the cab

window. "Probably got it tucked in the back of his pants."

Beau looked the man over from this distance. "This guy ain't shit."

Senior closed the door and climbed up in the bed, keeping his eyes always on the man. He unlocked a toolbox, moved some tools around, and came up with a tire iron and jack. The man was still staring down the highway. The man raised his hand above his brow. Senior looked down the highway at what had caught the man's attention. A vehicle was coming from the south in the distance. Senior hopped down back where Beau was standing. "Come on."

Senior and Beau began crossing the highway again toward the man. The man stood up on the bumper to look down the highway at the vehicle. "I think this is him. Yeah, it's him."

"That's him?" Senior shouted.

The man continued to look. "Yessir. Here he is. I told you not to bother." The man hopped off the trunk, still looking down the stretch at the vehicle. "Yep."

Senior and Beau continued to walk towards him. The vehicle was a truck, a late model pickup of a worn tannish hue with a long trucker's radio antenna flapping from the top of the cab.

Senior and Beau made it to Nicolas, "Thank you officers, I mean that, thank you very much. Sorry about all this. About you having to stop and all."

"Stop your apologizing mister, we were already driving by," Senior answered. "That's some kind of friend though."

The man nodded.

"What's his name?"

The man looked at Senior with some surprise.

"So I know who to thank."

The man continued to stare at Senior, "Miguel."

"Miguel. Thank you Miguel," Senior said.

The truck slowed, eventually pulling on to the shoulder and rolling in behind Senior's truck and trailer. There was only one man in the truck. He was much younger than Nicolas, perhaps in his late twenties. He was also Hispanic and had long, dark hair that rested past his shoulders. He was smiling at the group when the truck eventually came to a stop. The young man rolled down the window manually. "Nico, what kind of trouble you get yourself into here?"

Beau shouted back, "Your friend here bought a piece of shit with no tire!"

The driver sat in the cab smiling, "sounds about right."

Nicolas shouted at the man, "Sorry about all this!"

The driver smiled back at Nicolas and stared at him for a moment. The man then waved his hand in the air as if to brush away any cares, "I was just pissing the day away anyhow. Let me get my things."

The driver leaned over in the cab for a few brief moments, shuffling things about. He sat back up and opened the door and stepped out. He stepped to the side of the door and raised his hand quickly to eye level with something dark within its grip. A series of quick pops broke into the air as the man's hand gyrated violently. Beau flinched from the sudden noise, doubled over, and found himself hitting the ground flat on his back. Senior and Nicolas dropped heavy to the blacktop beside him within a second. Senior rolled on to his side toward Beau.

A darkness was washing over his chest and expanding. Beau looked to Senior's face – it was set to a shake. Several cracks continued to sound as strange whistles screeched continuously above and around Beau's head.

Beau lost his breath with the realization. He looked down at his own chest and began to feel about it. His hands were dry, there was no blood. Beau looked back up to the driver, he was walking across the highway changing the machine gun's clip, looking at Beau coldly. The horses in the trailer across the highway were squealing and panicking and banging about.

Beau sat up, unholstered his glock, pushed the safety out, and pointed at the man walking towards him in a motion so fluid it surprised him. Beau pulled the trigger once. The man's head whipped back, his knees buckled, and he fell on his side in the middle of the highway. Beau kept the glock leveled at the man on the ground. The horses continued to scream and bang against all sides of the trailer. Beau got to his knees and then stood all the way up. He walked toward the man with the glock pointed at the man's body. Beau glanced down at his own body as he continued to walk. There was no mark around him save for some grime from the asphalt.

Beau made it to the driver, looking down at him with the glock pointed at his face. The man's forehead was caved in. A black ooze of blood and matter poured out and ran all down his face, which could no longer be seen beneath it. Beau dropped his gun to his side and gasped, choking on the air itself. His stomach clinched and his throat restricted as he gagged, coughing and stumbling about. He found his knees with both hands and stabled himself as he bent over and continued to heave and cough every couple seconds. Spit projected from his mouth with each cough until there was no more to cough out.

The last sight of his father seized him.

Beau turned and began jogging back toward where Senior and Nicolas lay, wiping the spit from his face with his forearm sleeve, coughing all the time. Beau sidestepped Nicolas as he made for Senior's body. Nicolas' face, neck, and chest were shredded, his blood had already pooled around him all the way to where Senior lay. Senior was hunched over on his side from how Beau had left him. He was still.

Beau knelt down beside Senior and set the glock down on the blacktop. He took hold of Senior's shoulder to roll him over. Senior's shirt was sopped with blood that was warm to the touch. Beau gently rolled Senior onto his back. His face was pale. Blank. His mouth dropped open and remained ajar and loose. His eyes were half open and looking downward. He was no longer there. He was gone.

Beau let himself fall from kneeling back to sitting down on the asphalt. He looked away out to the horizon as a pain took hold of his chest. Telephone poles and their thick hanging wires set in front of the open desert plain beyond. A clear sky of a pure blue. Quiet. Beau did not look back down, but could feel his father heavy beside him all the same. The pain inside his chest became a burn which seemed to turn within him. Like a screw being driven down deep within. He put his hand on his chest over this spot and held it there. He kept on looking out at the empty plains. The world about him was as still and quiet as could be, and yet he could feel it changing in a violent fashion with each breath he took, though it seemed not to care a bit about such change. The sudden state of death, its weight, the bitterness of its abrupt grasp. He felt small, very small. He kept holding that spot of pain within him and knew that the world was not changing. It had not even noticed. It was him that wobbled. It was him that would change.

Beau looked to his other side where Nicolas lay, his body all broke and bloody. Beau raised himself up to his knees and crawled over to Nicolas' body. He reached into a front pocket on Nicolas' pants and took out his keyring. There was only one key and a cheap plastic key ring tag that read WESTSIDE MOTORS. Beau raised himself to standing, took a few steps to the trunk of Nicolas' car, and opened it. Nothing. The trunk was empty. Beau wiped his cheeks with the sleeve of his shirt. "That ain't the truth."

Beau began to feel about the edges of the carpet panel of the trunk floor until he got a grip at one of its sides. He lifted it up, pulled it out, and dropped it on the asphalt. A black duffle bag was stuffed down into the opening where the spare tire had been. "Uh huh." Beau unzipped the bag – it was full with money. Beau sifted through it to try to get a grasp at how deep it was stacked. Plenty deep past his elbow. Beau took his arm out and turned and looked back to the scene of the two dead men and his father. He sat down on the bumper and thought. He was surprised that no one had come upon the scene. He could not figure how much time had passed, but was surprised all the same. Like maybe the world had stopped altogether. Like maybe he was dead himself.

Beau turned back to the bag of money, reached in, and grabbed two armfuls. Stepping back and looking again at the money that remained in the bag, he saw he had taken about half or so. Beau looked down the highway in both directions. No cars, nothing. Beau crossed the highway and came to the back of the horse trailer. He set the money on the ground and unlatched the trailer doors. Both horses looked at him, blinking, standing still. Beau pushed his way past Senior's horse to the front of the trailer where the storage box was located. Beau emptied half of its fillings. He made two trips to pile the money at the bottom of the box. Beau filled the box over the money with the materials he had removed, closed the box, and walked back out of the trailer. He closed the trailer doors, but stopped short of latching them. He thought about what he had just done. He looked down at his boots. Dried blood was smeared all over the tops of them.

Beau locked the trailer up.

Beau walked back across the highway on his way to Nicolas' car to search it out more, though he did not have any further expectation. He walked by Senior's body almost to the car again. Beau stopped, not knowing really why. Beau looked back to Senior. Senior lay in the same position, but his head was tilted toward Beau, his eyes open and staring at him.

"Dad!" Beau hurried to Senior and dropped down beside him. Senior looked up at Beau with a focus about his eyes. Senior was not breathing and for a moment Beau still thought him dead. Senior raised his right hand, steady and untrembling. Beau was startled by the movement and leaned back. Senior was holding his set of keys, with one key singled out between his finger and thumb. Senior held it in the air as Beau looked on. Beau leaned over and took the key, feeling as he did that Senior's fingers were cold.

Senior's gaze focused all the more upon Beau. He took in a breath as if he knew it would be all he had, and spending such breath on the exhale he said as quick as he could: "I got a man locked away in the cellar but he ain't a man…" It was a quiet, fading tone, with his voice cutting off at the end of the statement with no more air to be found. He shook his head slightly left and then right and then left again. Senior tried to say something else and mouthed something twice, but Beau couldn't make it out.

Senior's eyes became still upon Beau. He let that be their final place. His stare rolled off his face as his eyes relaxed and fell out to nothing. He was gone once more. To where, Beau did not know, though he knew that it was far and that he would not again return.

- Beau

A week or so before Dad died, he got to talking about how this job was harder than it used to be. He said most people just don't believe in God anymore. Really believe in Him. Fear Him. Or fear themselves in light of Him.

He wasn't just talking about the worst of them. Though I've seen plenty of that sort. Men that have done awful things. Awful things. Some of them weren't men at all. One boy we caught up with down south of town was not but two weeks over fifteen. We pulled him over because he looked young, that was all. I thought maybe he had taken his daddy's car out. I'll tell you, I didn't sleep for three nights after I saw what he did to the man he crammed down in that trunk. You could ask Susie, I swear it, couldn't bring myself to much more than sit down. Him, I heard he slept sound as could be that very night. I'm sure he sleeps fine still.

Or these fellas that run drugs up from Palomas and Juarez. They would kill you without a care. Without a thought, you know? Six months back, a man and his boy hunting the antelope over by Tohachi came upon seven such men laid out across the mesa lands a couple miles off the highway. All shot to hell. The ugliest damn mess you could think of. We stared at them for a while, talked it over, took pictures. But really there wasn't much more that could be done than clean them up. I heard that next week that someone had caught up with another group of them up near Pueblo and left them in pieces. Somebody had to clean those boys up too. There's no sense to be made of it. Any of it. Don't bother yourself with trying.

But it's more than that. It's the regular folk too. Dad said he couldn't tell if it's that we don't want to believe in Him, or that we just don't care anymore. And those that say they do, well, many of them seem to have a god in mind that they made up in their own heads. Because if there's no true God, there's no such thing as sin, is there? And there are no consequences. Or real evil. And each person is a god unto themselves.

Dad said, he wondered how that shapes the world. Maybe harder isn't the way to put it. To be plain about it, he said, he was frightened of folks these days. A person that thinks they aren't tethered to something just doesn't see what it is they're now tethered to there in the dark they put themselves. And where it's pulling them. He said, there comes the worst of all his thoughts.

Beau laid in bed watching the ceiling fan twirl about in the shadows above him. He thought it strange, but its breeze brought something of a very real comfort to him, even as artificial and bland as it was. Its gentle hum something of a real isolation in this quiet room, where no other noise seemed able to exist. Its rhythmic cadence the only heartbeat in entirety, without meaning, without life behind it. Strange he thought. If he never left the moment, he would not have cared.

The morning light cut narrowly through the tops of the drapes. It dropped a line of gold across his bare chest. He followed the line across his chest with his fingertip until it reached its end above his heart. He laid his palm against the skin and waited to feel a heartbeat of his own. Nothing. Nothing. And then, a slow thump. Very slow. Deep. Warm. Imperfect rhythm. Alive. He could not hide from anything here, even for a short while.

The bedroom door opened. Susie leaned in and looked at him. She was wearing a black dress and held a hat under her arm. She walked in and came over to his side of the bed and sat down next to him. She placed her hand on top of Beau's hand, which still rested upon his chest. Her touch was warm. "It's probably about time," she said.

Beau looked at her hand resting atop his own. He put his other hand on top of hers and stroked the top of it with his thumb. "I know."

The church was full as could be. Every bit of the county that could have fit in the Southern Methodist was present. The men stood in the aisles and along the back and side walls, letting most every woman and child have a seat in a pew or foldup chair somewhere. Some people even stood outside watching through the windows. Reporters down from Albuquerque had been outside too, talking to people. Old women cried. Men shook their heads and cursed under their breath while talking with one another. The younger women held their children and told them things about heaven.

Reverend Blankenship began in his deep, monarchical tone. "The Gospel of John, Chapter 10. The Lord said, 'The thief comes only to steal and kill and destroy. But I came that the sheep may have life and have it abundantly.'" Reverend looked up and turned a somber gaze across the crowd, letting the quiet sit heavy upon the room as they all looked at him. He looked back down to the pulpit and began again. "'I am the good shepherd. The good shepherd lays down his life for the sheep. He who is a hired hand and not a shepherd, who does not own the sheep, sees the wolf coming and leaves the sheep and flees, and the wolf snatches them and scatters them. He flees because he is a hired hand and cares nothing for the sheep.'" Reverend looked up again at the crowd, commanding emphasis as he nodded slowly and looked over them. He looked down again. "'I am the good shepherd. I know my own and my own know me, just as the Father knows me and I know the Father; and I lay down my life for the sheep." Reverend paused for a moment, staring down at the pulpit still – "'No one takes it from me, but I lay it down of my own accord.'" Reverend again returned his gaze to the crowd. "'I lay it down of my own accord.' The word of the Lord."

And all the people replied, "Amen."

They buried Senior in the cemetery yard next to the church. Beau and five other deputies carried the casket across the yard directly, followed closely by the peoples who stumbled behind aimlessly like the mourning, whipped sheep personified. Senior's plot lay directly next to Sam Jr.'s, bringing something of a comfort, but with it also the edges of an old pain buried away for those that recognized it. When they began to lower the casket down into the hole, Beau's momma Jean wailed out and clutched Beau's shoulder, burying her head in his chest and closing her eyes tight with a cringe. She screamed. Screamed and bawled and yelled something out in between her breaths in a tongue indiscernible to all but herself. It was like no cry Beau had ever heard or seen. Not from his mother or any other soul. It scared him and he looked to Susie, who was bawling herself. Susie went and knelt down next to Jean on the other side and put her arms around her, laying her head onto the middle of Jean's back.

Senior's casket came to rest at the bottom of the grave. The lift made a jarring sound when it hit bottom like some door forever closing with a clang. People cried, but no one talked. It was silent for some five whole minutes. Reverend said a prayer. For Senior's soul. For Jean. For the church. For the people. For Beau, that he would be for them the "shepherd" that his father had been. Even as the words landed upon his ears, Beau knew that it would not be. He saw it plainly. It was already a thing which was gone. After an Amen from all, Reverend announced that there would be a brief reception with refreshments back in the church hall for everyone that wished to stay.

Everyone did stay and many stopped by to tell Jean or Beau or Susie something in regard to Senior. A story, a quote of some kind which had stuck, a joke, a regret. One man told Beau about how Senior had arrested him back in 92' when he was a young man and had provided the testimony that sent him to the penitentiary for three and one-half years. The man told Beau about how Senior had wrote him a note every couple months in prison and visited him when he was that way, telling him all about how he could turn it around. About how he had to turn it around. Senior had even given the man's wife some money a couple times when it had become real bleak. The man told Beau that when he got out, Senior had driven two hours to talk another man into giving him a job. A job which the man has never since left.

Beau excused himself and found his way to the steps

outside the back of the church. He sat down on the top step and rolled the tension out of his neck. He felt a discomfort at his hip from where the holster was clipped on the inside of his dress belt. It had rubbed some rawness into his side throughout the day. He unholstered the glock and held it out in front of him in his fingertips, with the handle within his left hand and the barrel within his right – feeling its weight, observing its smooth and dark contours, remembering what it could do, what it carried.

Beau set the glock down on the concrete next to his side. When he did, he saw a man standing a couple feet to his side at the top of the stairs, leaning up against the handrail. The man was old, seventy, with long white hair pulled back into a ponytail. He was Hispanic, his face of a worn and bronzed hue that had grown very dark over a life beneath the sun. He smiled at Beau with teeth that bore a light stain. He wore a black pin-striped suit, with a bolo tie hanging from his neck that was centered by a turquoise cattle skull. "Didn't mean to startle you."

"Oh, no, you didn't. I'm sorry. I'm all lost to thought these days."

"I doubt as if your thoughts are so lost as you might think. You mind?" the man asked while pointing down to a spot on the other side of the stair that Beau was seated upon.

As the man sat down, he cringed a bit with the creaks of his body until at last his rear reached the concrete. "Ah, hell. I'll tell you. One day you are a young man with all the strength of a bull," he said with a raised fist, "and then, well then the next you're that old dog on the corner of the porch that everyone hopes will die before it gets too bad," he finished while opening the fist and letting some invisible weight fall to the ground. "Listen to me, going on. Don't bother yourself with such things. You're a long way from the porch, eh."

"Sorry, I don't know if we've even met–"

"We haven't. And I would tell you my name if I knew you wouldn't forget it with the three dozen others that just got thrown on you back in there. Out of the woodworks they come, as they say."

"Did you know my father?"

"Knew, well, I knew of him. Like most. I don't believe we ever met though. My loss I'm sure."

"Paying respects then."

"Paying whatever I got to give. That's my generation though, you know? What we thought important, this new lot would not even recognize, or want for that matter. Respect. That is an idea that is dying with the old I think, I'm sorry to say."

Beau thought about that.

"There I go again huh. Sometimes the bullshit just falls right on out of my mouth. I won't feed you anymore of it. I'm not here to waste your time, or mine." The old man paused for a moment, as if to confirm within himself that what he said next was what he really wanted to say and that he was going to say it in the manner he wished. "As may have already crossed your mind, you weren't the only man to lose something out there on that highway."

"No?"

"No. You were not."

"What is it that you lost?"

The old man looked at him still as could be, waiting for

Beau to answer his own question.

"Is it that old man, what was it, Nicolas?"

"That dulce perro viejo? No." The man's face grew grave, taking the good-natured demeanor off like a mask removed. "I lost a son."

Beau noticed for the first time that the iris in the man's left eye had no color to it. Just a grayed, deadened shade.

"... And a half million dollars."

Beau sat back as the contours of this man, and his son, and his money came all into focus. Beau leaned over, grabbed the glock that lay between them on the concrete, and dragged it back to his side. The man did not flinch in the slightest and did not break his stare into Beau's eyes.

"Well," Beau began, "I'm sure you know I mean no disrespect to you personally mister when I say that I don't feel all that broken up about your boy. And as for the money, well, I do believe it has already been turned over to the county attorney. So you're going to have to talk to the judge about getting that back... aren't you."

A thin smile spread over the man's face. "I was talking about the other half million."

"Hell are you talking about–"

The man raised his hand to quiet him, "Don't. Don't do that."

Beau did just that. He offered not a word.

"Look here. I don't give a shit about that money. Understand? Drops in the bucket, eh. But what I do care very much about, and what I will not abide, is you. Is you having that money. You see? My son leaves that highway in a bag, his head all to mush. Your daddy leaves that highway in a bag, with not a drop of blood left in himself.

101

Even that sweetheart Nicolas leaves that highway in a bag. But you, you walk out a hero. A hero that is no hero at all. A thief. With my boy's blood underneath his boots."

The old man shifted his weight forward and reached into the front pocket of his suit coat. Beau raised the gun up at his side, not quite yet pointing it at the man. The man smiled as he saw this. The man reached into the pocket and pulled out a crumpled pack of cigarettes. He patted about his pants pockets until he found a lighter. "Curse of my family. All of us. The boy too." The old man lit up and sucked in the smoke deeply.

"You know, I thought for the first day or two that I might just let you keep that money. Let it eat at you as money with blood upon it does. Let the chips stay where they had fallen, you know? Shit, I bet you don't even know why you took it now that you look back at it. El terco burro that I am, I cannot leave it that way. Can't let the story end like that. You see, it's like these fables that I was told as a boy about the old legends of Mexico. A man was described always in such a light, with such heroics and valor and polished bullshit, you know? Nothing about the men that he had killed, or the women that he had used or worse, the children forgotten, or the things that had become his which were not," the man said, while waving his hand about in the air, sending trails of smoke every which way. "Even then, even as a boy, I knew that these men were not heroes. At least not all heroes, probably not even more so than not. I grew to hate them, as I grow to hate you even now," he said pointing two bony fingers at Beau which pinched the cigarette in between.

"Old man. What makes you think I could give a shit

about how you want this story to end?" Beau asked while punctuating the end of the sentence in the air with a slight point of the glock at the old man.

"Which is where this always ends," the man answered. "Unfortunately."

"How's that?"

"Threats. With me telling you how the men that came with me today are inside with your wife. With your mother. These are men that kill people for a living son. In all kinds of ways."

Beau looked back to the church, as if giving thought to getting up and making for the door.

"Nobody is getting hurt today. Least not if you keep that head on straight."

"You wouldn't. There'd be no end to them looking for you."

"I wouldn't? I am surprised that you would doubt such a thing, that is, if you really do. That is for the naïve. No, you are a man of this world. You have seen the things which take place. You should not ask yourself whether I would do such a thing. You do not know the man that sits before you. What you should ask yourself is, would the world allow such a thing? And you know the answer to that question."

Beau organized options in his head.

"This is normally the part where I would tell you it's just business. But that would be a lie in this case amigo–"

The back door to the church opened, cutting the man off. Susie appeared in the doorway with a face relieved to have found Beau.

"When did you run off? I thought you had left out for

home," Susie said as she walked toward them. "People are starting to leave."

The old man pushed himself up as she walked over and put a smile on his face. "So I'll come on by in the next couple days and pick it up. Sound good?" the man said casually as if he were speaking of a borrowed sweater. The man smiled kindly at Susie as he walked past her toward the church door.

Beau looked to the old man who was about at the door now. "What's your name? I won't forget it now."

The old man reached the door and pulled it open halfway. He turned, "Carlos. De Olmos." The man disappeared behind the shutting door.

"You ready to go? I want to go," Susie said, putting her hand on Beau's shoulder as he remained seated on the step.

"Baby, would you take Momma back to our place? Get her set up in the guest bed again. I got something I got to do."

"But I drove with you."

"I'll take her car. Meet you by dinner."

"You aren't coming back with us? She's a breath away from a breakdown Beau."

"I'll be around soon. Please."

Beau drove his mother's car to his parents' ranch home outside of town. There was an overcast on the afternoon, rendering the world about in a sulkened state. The ranch home itself seemed to wear this somber tone by its lonesome at the end of the long country road. Beau pulled the car into the driveway and stepped out. He walked to the fence at the end of the driveway and stared out at the barn some fifty yards out on the land. Although the barn appeared much as it had since he was a boy, he noticed now for the first time that the front of the barn looked like some primitive face shouting. The two round window shutters on the second floor a set of artificial, beady eyes, the wide rectangular door a great opened mouth set to a yell. He pulled Senior's keys out from his jacket pocket and found the particular key that Senior had picked out moments before he passed. It was a small key, likely to some type of padlock.

Beau walked down the dirt path to the barn much the same as he had a thousand times since his boyhood. In his right hand he held Senior's keyset with the key singled out between his thumb and finger. In his left, an electric lantern. When he reached the barn, he walked around to its rear. The cellar was something of an old emergency shelter built down under the barn itself, with its door established out on the ground behind the barn. The heavy iron door had always been closed with a latch when he was a boy, but never with a lock. It now was. A heavy duty, industrial padlock of solid steel clasped the latch down secure.

Beau set the lantern down and took hold of the padlock. The outside of the lock had been weathered some by seasons past, though not many from the looks of it. Beau inserted the key and turned till it popped open. As it did, Beau thought of his father's face as it had been when he was laid out on the highway. As he had died. Beau slipped the lock off of the latch and held it within his hand, looking at it. He had never heard his father say something that was not true.

Beau lifted the iron door up and swung it over on its hinges until he could rest it on the ground without it slamming. A warm and acrid must poured out from the dark opening and washed over his face. Beau turned and brought his forearm up over his nose and mouth until the trapped air had escaped into the world above. Beau stepped toward the opening and looked down into the darkness. The stairs leading down under the barn quickly disappeared from the light of the world and beyond all sight. Beau knelt down and listened. There was no sound to be heard. He waited for nearly five minutes, but there was no change. Beau could not decide if that was a good or bad thing.

Beau stood back up. As he stared down into the opening, he could see his shadow cast upon the stairs that remained in the light. A man alone on the path into an awaiting dark which would swallow him. Beau picked up the electric lantern at his feet and turned it on. The thought again arose that he had never heard his father say something that was not true. This set his heart to racing. Beau took the first step down. He followed each next step slowly, one-by-one, with every intention of not making any noise himself.

The wood stairs creaked with each step Beau took like muffled moans in the quiet. Beau held the lantern out in front of him as far as he could, casting a blurred gray upon the dirt floor of the cellar. The sour taste of the must around him grew heavier it seemed with each breath, with each step. Beau stopped this slow creep when he reached the bottom of the stairs. He held out the lantern and squinted and listened.

The place was utter dark outside the edges of the lantern's grayed beam. The cellar was as long as the barn itself, and though the lantern illuminated its other end to some degree, it did so in a partial and murky fashion. There were no objects around him directly. Nothing stored. Beau expected such as Senior never came down here. He could not remember exactly the last time he had been here either. There was however the dark outline of something at the end of the cellar, tall and protruding and undeniable.

Beau walked slowly toward the object. The dirt of the cellar floor crackled underneath each step. As Beau came within twenty feet of the object, he could see that it was a large black metal box of about seven feet tall. Maybe four, four and-a-half feet wide. He stopped and looked at it more. There were thick chains wrapped tightly around the middle of the box as if it were wearing them as a belt. Beau walked closer until he was standing directly in front of the box. He lifted the lantern up over his head to cast light on it entirely. It was made of a heavy metal, maybe cast iron, and was of industrial quality. It seemed to be some type of locker, as it had a door at its front with a handle, which was what the chains were fastening shut. Beau now saw that a padlock identical to the one on the cellar door above locked the heavy chains in place.

Beau scanned his gaze down the locker from its top. Beau noticed now that there were four horizontal slits of about a half-inch or so thick at the middle of the locker door. He shifted the angle of the lantern downward to let light into the slits - *two eyes looked out at him from the top slit* – the sight stabbed a chill through to Beau's heart as if on the tip of a dagger. Beau jerked back and ended up on his rear on the dirt. "Holy shit! Shit!" Beau shouted as he scrambled backwards on his rear in the dirt, "the hell, shit!"

Beau stopped scrambling after four or five feet. Dust was swirling in the air around the locker inside the lantern's beam.

Air returned to Beau's lungs gradually. Moments of quiet followed as the dust continued to swirl in the light. He raised the lantern to cast light upon the slits on the face of the locker. The eyes were fixed upon him.

The question felt stupid even as it was loaded in his mouth, but he could think of no other, "somebody in there?" Something shifted its weight in the locker. The eyes appearing in the slit disappeared with the shifting. Chains rattled from inside. The eyes again appeared, peering out at him, taking him in.

Beau got to his feet and turned for the stairs. He ran for the stairs with the lantern shaking violently at his side, casting wild flashes about the cellar with each step. Beau knew not exactly why he ran, or why he was so frightened in the moment, though such questions did not slow him. Each stair banged as he ran up towards the daylight, his run ever increasing until he was in the light.

CHAPTER 12 – THE MAN

They sat around the kitchen table eating in the quiet. Beau and Susie ate left over finger foods from the funeral reception earlier in the day. Empanadas filled with chorizo and green chili. Black beans. Mexican rice with spiced bits of chicken. They drank punch that Reverend had poured into a washed out milk jug. Beau's momma Jean could eat none of it and instead drank warmed tomato soup from a mug.

Beau built a fire in the living room fireplace of pinon wood from the porch and all retired to the couches by the fire. No one turned on the television and no one asked to turn on the television. Beau sat back in his reclining chair, but did not prop up his legs. Susie sat on the end of the couch with Jean laying out on the rest of the couch and resting her head on Susie's lap. Susie pet her hair gently. They sat in the quiet watching the fire burn away, listening to it pop and sizzle and hiss. Jean began to cry and sobbed for a half hour on Susie's lap. Susie continued to stroke her hair and would rub her back in slow circles off and on. Beau looked on. With nothing to say he said nothing. Sometime shortly after her crying Jean fell asleep right there in Susie's lap.

Beau and Susie kept to the night's silence for some time after. Watching the fire. Watching the wood lose its form under the pressure of the fire.

"She's going to be okay," Susie said with a reserved voice, continuing to stroke Jean's hair as she lay asleep on her lap.

"I don't doubt that she'll go on all right in time," Beau

said, pausing to further construe his prediction of the sleeping widow's future, his mother's future. "But she isn't ever going to be okay."

Susie looked down at Jean's face to see if such a prediction fit. "I don't know," she said. "You think she should come stay with us for good?"

"I think we should offer it. But she would never do such a thing. She just wouldn't."

Susie thought about that and looked on at the fire. She seemed to be thinking deeper about it than the comment allowed for on its face. "The wages of sin. A peculiar thing," she said.

The firewood hissed as Beau thought about this statement. "What do you mean?"

"You never heard that phrase?"

Beau thought again. "Wages and sin?"

Susie looked out on the fire, not volunteering an explanation on her own for a bit.

"It's from one of Paul's letters. And it isn't 'wages and sin,' it's the wages of sin," she said.

"Okay then."

"As Paul said, a couple times I think, the wages of sin are death. That's what you get from it. Period, no way around it. Death in this world and the one to come he says," she continued.

"That's not all that peculiar."

"I was thinking, looking here, that ain't it peculiar who often receives such wages?"

Beau looked at his momma sleeping there, with a dried stream of tears down her cheek having turned a red with irritation.

"Of course it usually is that person, but it most never is only that person is it," Susie continued, "it was Senior. It's Momma now. Us. We are all of us receiving these wages, aren't we? Death in full or in part. All because of that man's sins." She sighed in the middle of her train of thought as a realization must have taken hold of her, "And had the good Lord not forbade it, it would have been you in a box too." She thought on that and shook her head with a tremble as if she had felt a chill run through her body. "Thank the Lord."

"I see what you're getting at. I do. But no one else would have got anything from that man's sins if they hadn't chosen to."

"What?"

"You don't see it? Dad chose to be the law. Chose to stop on that highway. Chose to be the symbol that man shot at, to put himself in such affairs. So did I. So did you by becoming part in me, as did Momma some time ago with Dad," Beau paused, adding all this up in his head. "See? We have always been in line for such things, probably lucky they hadn't come yet."

"That don't change anything."

"No?"

"It didn't when it came to Christ, did it?" she asked.

Beau thought on that as well. "I'm not tracking I guess."

"He chose to come down and to 'put Himself in such affairs' as you say. But as sure as day He was receiving the wages of all us and none of His own on that cross. His choosing to be there didn't change the owner of those wages did it? Only their destination. His choice to be such a receptacle, for the good mind you, ain't no different in kind than what your daddy's was in showing up on that highway."

Beau did not have a reply to offer as he thought over the contours of this while looking on at his wife and mother glow from the shine of the fire.

"Senior only chose the good, and that choice was all by itself good,'" she continued. "And that's my point. Isn't it peculiar that those who choose the good often receive a collateral payment in such wages? Maybe the direct payment, who knows? Maybe it has to be that way. It was true for Christ. Probably so for your daddy, though I can't figure it."

Beau and Susie remained quiet for five whole minutes staring on at the fire. Quiet all but for the pop and hiss of the fire itself. Thoughts diverging within their minds on two separate trails. Thoughts of themselves. Thoughts of God Almighty. Thoughts of Senior in the ground, and where else he might be at that very moment.

Beau looked to her. "You know how much I love you, right?"

"I do."

Beau came and picked up Jean from off of Susie's lap and carried her upstairs like a worn child in his arms and laid her in the guest bed. He tried to pull the covers over her but she awoke and refused to go to sleep in the black dress and told him that she could now put herself to sleep though she thanked him all the same.

Susie was in the shower when Beau came to their bedroom. Beau took off his clothes and stepped in with her. She washed his hair out with soap and scrubbed his back. He turned and held her and they kissed with that love that grows within the covenant deep as marrow. He held her again for a short time as the warmth of the water washed over them entire.

Susie read the Bible from bed for some minutes and then spent some less minutes in the middle of a novel about a sheriff of the old frontier until her eyes were heavy beyond her liking. Beau laid on his pillow and stared up at the slow moving ceiling fan, which Susie preferred always on, on account of the hum it provided the room.

"You ready to put the lights out?" she asked.

Beau was away somewhere in thought as he looked on at the fan.

"Hun?" she asked again.

Beau heard her this time and snapped to, looking over at her. "Hmm?"

"You ready to go to sleep?"

"Oh. Yeah."

"I can leave the light on if you want, I don't mind."

"No. No, that's okay, I'm ready."

"Okay then," she said. Susie rolled toward the nightstand and turned off the lamp. "Good night," she said in a quieter tone in the dark.

"Good night."

Susie rolled over in the covers facing him and rested her head on the pillow and closed her eyes. "Beau?" she asked with her eyes still closed.

"Uh huh?"

"I'm so sorry about daddy."

Beau turned over and rubbed the length of her arm over the covers.

They fell quiet for several minutes in the dark, Susie appeared to fall off to sleep. Beau stared on at the ceiling fan still off in some thought unknown to her.

From the quiet she spoke again, "Beau?"

"Uh huh?"

"Who was that man you were talking to outside of church today?"

"What man?"

"The old man with the suit. The one you were talking to when I came out and got you to leave."

Beau was quiet for a moment. "I don't know who he is."

"What did he want?"

Beau was quiet for a moment longer. "Some money."

"Why would he want money from you?"

"I don't know," he said. "He was confused I think."

"Were you able to set him straight?" she asked still with eyes closed.

"If I didn't, then I soon will."

She was quiet for a moment, maybe having fallen to sleep. "Okay," she said and then she spoke no more.

Beau stared on at the ceiling fan into the middle of the night some three hours longer until he could lie there no more. He looked over at Susie sleeping. A soul at peace with itself if ever there was one. Beau got out of bed without stirring her and went to the closet and got dressed in the dark.

Beau went downstairs without turning on any lights and went to the refrigerator. Beau pulled out the almost empty plastic jug of punch that Reverend had given them and washed it out under the faucet. Upon draining it twice,

Beau let the gallon fill with water and then screwed the cap upon it. Beau brought the jug with him and went to the garage. He searched through a chest of materials until he found a large funnel he planned to use for draining oil still brand new and in its package. Beau retrieved the funnel and jug, opened and closed the garage door by hand so as to not make any noise, got in his truck, and set out down the driveway and into the road and into the night.

Beau stood looking down at the cellar door on the ground made visible by the grayed beam of the electric lantern. The night's dark and quiet was set around the barn and this door deep and resonant. His parents' ranch was isolated from the world by more than the miles of desert to the next ranch home. A spot in God's world isolated from all things comforting and alive. At least in his own mind. Beau unlocked the padlock on the cellar door and swung the door over on its hinges to rest on the ground. The must put a sick feeling to his stomach. Beau picked up the funnel and jug of water, securing the jug underneath his arm. He held the lantern out and walked down the stairs into the earth.

He stopped at the bottom of the stairs and looked out at the dark figure of the locker at the other end of the cellar. He took in a deep breath of the must and walked towards it. He directed the beam of the lantern toward the middle of the locker's face where he now knew the slits to be. When he got within ten feet of the locker, he could see the eyes looking out at him from the top slit half-way up the face of the locker door. Beau stopped and stared back. Beau's breath was loud amidst the quiet.

The raspy voice of a man came forth, "He is dead

then."

"What?" Beau asked.

"Those keys in your hand there," the voice responded. "The old man that gave them to you."

Beau looked to his hand and the keys. Silence settled for a moment. Beau held out the lantern and walked closer to the locker, stopping five feet short. "I got some water here." Beau set the jug down on the ground and rested the funnel on top of it.

"Not all boys look like their fathers, but you, you look like him. I see him standing there. I do."

Beau lifted the lantern higher, trying to play the angle of the beam into revealing more through the slit from his vantage point. The face around the eyes was made of a dark-tan skin, but the rest of the face was but shadow that could not be seen, with the only discernible feature being the bridge of the man's nose.

"How did he die?" the voice asked.

Beau stood thinking of what to say, if anything at all, looking at those eyes.

"What's your name?" the voice asked again.

"Why are you here like this?" Beau finally responded.

The man in the locker looked into Beau's eyes as if fixed on something behind them.

"Locked up like this. What did you do to make him put you here?" Beau asked. "This ain't him."

"I don't think we have much to say to each other, you and I," the man responded. "You didn't come down here to let me out."

Beau stared back into the eyes. He wondered how they saw him.

"Not yet you didn't," the man said. "You just want to see if it's true."

Beau shifted the lantern to his other hand and recentered it to see the man's eyes again.

"Whatever it is he told you. Whatever it is he believed," the man said.

There was again what felt like a long silence between the two.

"You don't want this water here, do you?" Beau asked.

The eyes did not blink. Beau did not think he had seen them blink yet. Beau could not remember the last time he felt it hard to keep on looking into a man's eyes. Whether it was the circumstances, or whatever else was at work, there was a subtle pain in Beau's chest from staring at them. It would not let him breathe comfortably.

"You going to tell me what this is all about?" Beau asked again.

"It will reveal itself in time. I'm sure of it," the man replied. "I thought I was here to teach your father something. But then, here you are." The man paused a moment longer. "I guess it's you then."

"He told me to kill you," Beau replied.

The man's eyes leveled, as if this brought him a smile.

"I have most always done what he told me to," Beau said.

"Boy. You are nothing like him. You never will be."

Beau bent down and took hold of the jug of water in one hand. Still bending down, he secured the lantern under his armpit so as to unscrew the top of the jug with the other hand. When it was done, he adjusted so that the lantern was held out in one hand and the jug in the other, still bending down low, shining the lantern down at knee level with the jug. Beau began pouring the water out slowly onto the gravel. Short, cyclical gurgles came from the jug as the water fell out of the mouth of the jug and splashed onto the gravel. Beau kept looking down at the jug, letting it run slow for the man to see. When it was finally empty, Beau turned it over entirely to let the last few droplets of water drip out, shaking the ones that would not come voluntarily. When it was done, he secured the jug under his armpit once more to screw the cap back on. He grabbed the lantern with his other hand again and stood up to look to the man – but as he held out the lantern, the dark figure of a shadowy hand reached out from just beyond the lantern, shooting past the lantern to grasp for the center of his chest – the shock and sudden horror of which knocked him backwards, causing him to scream out as he fell.

Beau hit the ground hard. He shuffled backwards on the gravel, feeling about his chest frantically. After he had scooted several feet, he stopped, feeling about his chest more slowly. Though this dark hand had appeared to reach straight into his chest, he never felt it. Felt nothing. He caught his breath on the ground and listened. Quiet and nothing more. The lantern was on its side several feet in front of him, still on and shining out into the dark. The tall figure of the locker towered from out past the lantern. The man was quiet. Beau got to his feet and walked back over and picked up the lantern at the spot that he had fallen from. He raised the lantern again to shine onto the narrow slits and the man's eyes. They looked at him. Quiet still. Beau's breath slowed as he looked on.

"You aren't like him," the man said again in his dry, rasped tone. "You don't even want to be."

Beau stayed quiet. The eyes disappeared below the slits. The sounds of chains dragging against the inside of the locker screeched as the man slid down. The sound of weight came to rest as the man reached the bottom of the locker. Quiet fell heavy once more. Beau listened.

Beau backed away a few steps, looking at the locker still. He turned to walk to the stairs – a thunderclap rang out from inside the locker – some immense strength crashing upon the wall of the locker's inside. It stopped Beau in mid-step and put a still to his heart like a small child's when his father screams out. Beau stood still for a moment as the clang drowned out into the darkness around him. He began to walk again.

"If I were you," the man said in a muffled voice from down in the locker, pausing to see if Beau would stop. Beau did, the crackles created by his steps on the gravel ceasing. "I wouldn't take anyone I loved with me where I was going."

Beau stood for a moment to see if the man would say anything else. He did not. Beau began to walk again, each step crackled with the gravel. As Beau made it to the stairs, he hurried his walk up until he could feel the cold of the night air upon his face.

Beau slipped back into bed beside her. Though she was rolled over the other direction he could tell that she was awake by her breathing. The clock beside her read 2:47 in a lime neon. She did not ask him where he had been.

Beau was able to fall asleep within a half hour. It was a troubled sleep which wrapped around him like a fever. He dreamed of dreaded things in shadows groping after him. Of drowning deep down in the dark of some place in some thick substance of a frigid cold that was not water. Of some presence bearing down upon him which left him paralyzed and without any ability to brace himself for the coming pain. Of things which sparked fears and excitements which he recognized even as they happened could only exist within a dream. When he was let go from such dreams, he opened his eyes to his bedroom, which looked like a place he had not seen for some long time and could barely recognize himself within it. Susie's clock read 9:23, with the daylight pouring in through the window by the bed.

She had left a note on the kitchen table that her and Jean had left out for the store. There were grits in a bowl in the refrigerator covered by a paper towel. Beau ate the grits cold and drank a glass of milk and left out for the day.

- Beau

Momma and I were sitting out on the porch one Sunday afternoon after church in the summertime. This was when I was a boy. She was reading her Bible on the bench swing. I was playing with toys on the ground.

She began to read aloud, "James 1.   Son, you listening?"

I looked up at her.

She began again, "When tempted…"   She stopped and looked down at me again.   "You know what tempted means, don't you?"

"I think so."

"What does it mean?

I thought on it a bit.   "Tempted is like, when you want something.   When you want something you're not supposed to."

"Yeah," she said.   "That's right."

She looked back to the Book.   "When tempted, no one should say, 'God is tempting me.' For God cannot be tempted by evil, nor does he tempt anyone; but each person is tempted when they are dragged away by their own evil desire and enticed."

She stopped again.   "Enticed is like tempted.   Drawn to something.   You understand?"

"I think so."

She looked back again to the Book and read the next sentence more carefully.   "Then, after desire has conceived, it gives birth to sin; and sin, when it is full-grown, gives birth to death."

She looked back to me again. Reading my face. Measuring whether I understood. She patted a spot next to her on the bench. I got up and sat down beside her. "What's that on your shirt there?" she asked, looking at my shoulder.

I looked and saw that there was a number of balls of cottonseed from the cottonwood trees around the yard that had landed and stuck on my shirt. I picked at one of them until I had it between my fingers. I looked to the air around the porch and saw that these balls of cotton swirled all about.

Momma took the cotton from my hand and looked it over. "This is how it starts. Like a seed."

Momma let the cotton go into the air. It caught the breeze and blew off the porch out into the yard. "Anyone can get rid of it if they want to. If they choose to. They just got to let go."

Momma nodded out to the group of cottonwoods that grew at the sides of the driveway up the yard. "Seeds only do one thing son and that's grow. You let sin catch root and before you realize it'll dig its way down deep into you. And it'll grow and spread out all over your life with its anchors down in you. Until it's part of who you have become. By then you won't even recognize it to be a separate part from you. By then you won't want to. You won't see it for what it is. What it has always been."

She nodded at those trees again.

"You ever known a person that could move a cottonwood?" she asked.

"No Momma," I said.

"The good Lord, there hasn't ever been sin he could not root out in saving someone. But I'll tell you. It ain't a regular thing for a person to ask once such a thing is full grown and set."

It was quiet between us. The cottonseed filled the air.

"Most people just stay put. Die under their trees," Momma said.

Beau sat in what had been his father's office filling out paperwork regarding his interim appointment as Sheriff that had to go before the council in their afternoon meeting. He was in plain clothes and did not plan to stay beyond an hour as he was off on leave for the rest of the week.

Beau set down the pen and looked over the office. Most everything was as his father had left it. The air carried something of his presence yet. Beau turned in the chair, looking around it all in the quiet. He saw on the wall above and behind the desk that framed piece of scripture that had been hanging on the very spot since he was a boy. Grandad gave it to Senior upon his election to Sheriff long ago and it has remained. Psalm 9.

> Arise O Lord! Let not man prevail;
>> Let the nations be judged before you!
> Put them in fear, O Lord!
>> Let the nations know that they are only men!

Senior sat beneath it all Beau's life.

The office door opened. Rebecca leaned in, "Sorry to bother, I know that you aren't even supposed to be here, but I got a gentleman from the DEA over in Tucson that would like a word with you."

Beau signed on the supervisor's line, checked to make sure there were no other such spots to be signed, and looked up at her. "Can you have Coleman take him, I really shouldn't get involved in anything until everything gets finalized, you know?"

"I know all that, but he wasn't asking to talk to the Sheriff. He was asking for you specifically."

"Oh." Beau looked to the watch on his wrist. "All right then, patch him through I guess."

"Oh, no, I mean I got him right out here in the lobby."

Beau leaned and looked out past Rebecca to the lobby and saw the man sitting there across the room in a chair with a file resting on his lap. Beau lowered his voice. "Did you know he was coming in today?"

"Sure didn't. He just showed up a couple minutes ago."

Beau looked at his watch again. Beau pushed the files toward the edge of his desk, "Okay then, send him in. And can you go ahead and hold on to these and get them filed after they wrap everything up this afternoon?"

Rebecca walked over and took the files from the desk, "Sure thing." She walked out of his office, leaving the door open. Beau could hear her inviting the man back.

The man walked into Beau's office with a cordial, but serious expression upon his face. He was middle-aged, very much overweight, and had a flat-top crew cut which looked military. He wore khaki pants and a tucked-in navy blue polo shirt with his gun and badge attached to his belt, which wrapped the circumference of his large belly. A distinct tan line from sunglasses rested around his eyes. "Beau Williams?" he asked as he stepped into the doorway.

"Yessir," Beau replied, standing to shake the man's hand.

"Can I?" the man asked pointing to the door.

"Go ahead."

The man closed the door and walked over to Beau's desk and extended his hand. "Dan Stills. I'm with the DEA office out in Tucson."

Beau shook his hand. "Becky told me. What can I do for you?"

"I'm going to sit down, is that all right?"

Beau nodded and the both of them sat. The man exhaled deeply with a sigh as if letting out pressure that had been building upon his mind. "I appreciate you seeing me here. I was actually out at your house a half hour ago. Must have missed you."

"My house? I apologize if I missed a message from you or something, I'm not sure Becky told you, I've been out."

Stills nodded his head, thinking it seems about this statement. "When was the funeral?"

"Yesterday."

"Yesterday." The look in Stills' eyes seemed to show him picturing what such a funeral must have looked like. "No. I didn't call. I didn't leave any messages."

Beau thought on that. "What can I do for you?"

"Is it all right if I call you Beau?"

"Sure."

"Beau, I'm going to do you the respect of not beating around the bush with you here. I would appreciate you showing me the same courtesy. I know you know all this, but I got to say it anyway, I'm here to ask you some questions about that whole mess out there on the highway. You don't have to answer them, but I would suggest that you do. I would hope that you take my driving all the way out here as both a sign of how serious I am, but also about me giving you the benefit of the doubt."

The edges of the situation fell into place as Beau stared at the man, suddenly conscious of his own facial reaction and that this man was studying it. That he had been since he walked into the room.

"Benefit of the doubt as to what?" Beau asked.

"Nicolas Corrales."

"Was that the man who drove the car, or the one who drove the truck?"

Stills grimaced as if this statement had caused him something of a physical pain. "Now let me stop you right there before we get started off on the wrong foot and you misunderstand me. I have your statement in this folder right here, this one right here, and know well enough that you know who Nicolas was. So this playing coy shit right off the bat is pissing me off a little bit and I feel like I need to remind you again that I drove out personally to sit here in front of you. Drove out here by myself. Understand? Don't prove me wrong before we even get to the hard questions."

Beau's silence and expression conceded his understanding.

"Corrales was an informant of ours. Had been for the last seventeen months. He was connected, albeit down the line a ways, from what we believe to be a substantial mover in these parts on over to California. As you know by now, one of his jobs was that of money mover." Stills opened his file and shuffled several pages until he picked out one and placed it in front of Beau on the desk. Beau looked it over. It was a spreadsheet with corresponding dates, locations, and amounts. Amounts. Beau's stomach tightened.

Stills continued, "this was a running tally provided by Corrales of all the money he was moving, or was about to move. Look at that last line Beau. What does it say?"

Beau took time to read it again, and then again. "Do you want me to read it out loud?"

"I know what it says."

"What do you want me to do?" Beau asked.

"I want you to tell me how in the hell I reconcile that with what else I got in here. With what else you said in your statement."

"That you got a rotten informant? That he was playing up numbers on you to make him seem that he was more important than he was. That he..." Stills' face cringed again and he lifted his hand to stop Beau, but Beau kept on, "... that he was lying to you. What?"

Stills slammed his raised hand down onto Beau's desk and let the sound of it settle into the air while he kept his face cringed, trying to recompose himself in his own mind.

"I am here by myself. Why do you think that is?"

"Mr. Stills, I can't tell you why that is."

"468,000 dollars." Stills let that settle too. "That's what's gone. And hear me. For what Corrales had at stake, he has never lied to me."

Beau sat back in his chair. Organizing options beneath the rising pulse of panic. "What do you want?"

"Well it ain't you. Understand? So what else is there?"

Beau stared at Stills, not wanting to finish what was hanging in the air from this question.

"Give me that money. Look, I can't say it any plainer than this, I'm here by myself. See? There is no one else that knows but me and you. Give me that money and I'll stop this train before it ever gets going."

Beau stared on, still not biting on what he knew could be the hook which ended his very life.

Stills continued, "Or else you'll be giving it to me once the train comes clear off its tracks. And it won't be just me anymore. And there won't be anyone that can help you. Sure as hell not me."

Beau stayed quiet. Before him were two paths. One in which this man Stills was something of a savior. The other in which he was the executioner himself wearing a savior's wrappings. Beau knew that there weren't really two paths, but only one which actually existed, with the other either a figment of deception to lead him to the noose, or a figment of fear that would keep him from pulling his head out of the noose already tightening. What could not be denied is that he was at this path's edge and felt now in that moment as it had presented itself that there was but no other path to be walked. Savior or no savior. For if Stills was the executioner, he would be so always and the path to destruction would be Beau's lot whether or not it was by his own choosing.

"Start with this," Stills said as he went back into his folder and pulled out a picture and laid it down on the desk. "Take me to this trailer." The photograph was of the highway and Senior's horse trailer as it had appeared that day hitched behind Senior's truck. There were bloodied outlines of partial footprints on the blacktop that led across the highway and to the back of the trailer. The ones Beau himself had left. Stills looked at Beau and then used two fingers like imaginary legs to walk the trail of the footprints across the photograph to the trailer.

"You drive," Stills said.

Beau and Stills drove out of the station lot and through the town toward its outer edge. Beau knew not what to say to the man. Stills looked out the window surveying the town as if he were on a casual drive with an old friend and there was not a care on his mind. At the least, such quiet was not a bit heavy to him. Beau felt its bearing however, the silence itself his admission and conviction entire.

They soon reached the edge of town and began down the country road which would after five or so miles lead to a true dirt and patch road which would lead to the ranch. Every half mile or so a stop sign would halt their drive at the T of the next intersecting ranch road. After two such stops, Stills looked over to Beau. He stared at him for a moment before speaking. "I don't think of you as a bad man. For what it's worth," Stills said.

Beau looked to him as he accelerated from the stop to the slow pace at which he drove the road. Beau looked back to the road without response.

"I don't," Stills continued. "I've been a witnessing party to a heavy share of shit in my day. Shit that just don't make sense except for the evil about the people involved."

Beau continued to look out onto the road in silence.

"But this," Stills began again, "this makes sense to me. My Lord, I don't think I have ever heard of a son seeing such a thing happen to his daddy. In those circumstances, with such an opportunity riding about the neck of such a tragedy. With the law all behind you and nobody else about you except the ones effecting the tragedy. And with it being their spoils yet. No, no, I don't think there is much precedent to judge from at all."

Beau continued on driving without saying a thing. The quiet between them resumed. The sound of the heavy truck rolling over gravel and dirt and country filled the cab. The next stop sign appeared out ahead at the next T. Beau pumped the breaks as he slowed them until he stopped altogether before the sign. Beau sat for a moment with the engine idle, looking down at the steering wheel as if somewhere within it was his answer for himself. Stills looked on, anticipating the response coming. Beau kept quiet and thinking, sitting there and running through it all in his mind. The moment became a minute with Beau keeping to this quiet, staring down. Stills sat quiet too, with Beau feeling his eyes upon him and waiting, but without impatience to rush a response to such thoughts.

Who knows what Stills thought. He could have been laughing up there in that head of his just the same as if his heart were actually broken for the man.

Movement caught the corner of Beau's eye at the driver side window beside him. He turned and saw a man standing at the window with a pistol pointed at his face three inches behind the glass. A thunderclap ripped the air around him and into his ears something awful and jolted Beau to shock. Beau's vision cut to white for a flash – when it cut back to the world from wherever it had gone Beau saw the same man pointing the gun at him behind the window with the window yet still intact. The man's face was enraged and shouting something at him though Beau could not hear a thing. There was a smattering of dark spots of some thickness spread out on the inside of the window now. The thick and dark substance of these spots ran down each from its origin. Beau felt a hotness about the back of his head and shoulder.

Beau turned back toward where Stills sat, seeing as he did this dark substance sprayed across the inside of the windshield and dash. A baseball-sized hole was blown out through the middle of the windshield itself. When Beau's eyes met back with the passenger seat he saw another man dragging Stills' body out of the truck from the passenger door. Stills' face was all but gone and replaced by a bloodied mush, and as his limp body turned from being pulled out, a large hole was revealed at the back of his head. Shattered glass from the passenger window and windshield was strewn about everywhere with pieces of Stills himself.

Beau felt a tug at his arm and then a stronger pull until he was out of the truck from his own door and falling down onto the dirt. "Levantate perra," a voice yelled at him. "Levantate! Levantate! Get up! You get up!" the man yelled again as Beau looked around still dizzied from the onset of all this. There were now two SUVs pulled in behind Beau's truck. Five or six men were standing there looking down at him while two others were lifting Stills' body into position to throw him into the bed of Beau's truck. The man beside Beau pulled him up by his shoulders until he took over and stood up himself. "Hey!" The man grabbed Beau's pistol from off of his side and took it in his other hand. The man then grabbed hold of Beau's face in his hand. "Despierta gringo." The man turned Beau's face to the left where he saw that De Olmos was walking towards him. De Olmos was wearing a white t-shirt, jeans, and boots of a dark leather. He had on a worn cowboy hat of a tan hue with his long white hair hanging free to his shoulders. He was looking toward Beau's feet as he came.

"Lean em' up against the truck here," De Olmos said. "Go on, lean him up right here."

The man jabbed the point of the pistol sharply into Beau's chest and pushed him backward until he was leaning against the truck. De Olmos walked up directly in front of him and looked at him with something of pity.

"What were you doing?" De Olmos asked in a soft tone.

Beau stood blinking at him. He had caught up to his breath and was snapping back to by the moment.

"Huh?" De Olmos asked again.

"I, I, don't know. We were driving, I, was driving," Beau muttered, still coming back together.

"Let go of the man," De Olmos said to the man that had been holding Beau up with the pistol driven home in Beau's chest. "Go on." The man pushed Beau upright completely against the side of the truck and then stepped back with the pistol coming down to his side. The truck shook as the other men dropped Stills' body down into the bed. Beau looked over and down at him, the blood running still from all parts of it. A thing so quick no longer human. Meat and mess and no soul.

"This was your way out? I wasn't going to do anything about it?" De Olmos asked, catching Beau's eyes back to himself.

"No. No I didn't think anything," Beau replied.

"You got this man here killed. I didn't want to kill anybody."

"He showed up all on his own. He was on to it all on his own."

De Olmos looked into Beau's eyes, measuring it. "And you were taking him to my money?"

Beau looked back at him, the answer hanging clear.

"At that ranch of your daddy's?"

Beau looked at the other men standing by and staring, each with a glare as cold as could be. Men of Mexico's border, a part in those things which she permits there. He knew then that he was dead and that he would not see Susie again and that she would be by herself worrying about him and praying about him and mourning him until she was sick. And him somewhere out in a hole in the desert. And her knowing that down in her heart. And her not knowing why, except that he could not have wound up there unless he was not the man she thought he was.

"Don't look at them," De Olmos said.

Beau looked to the old man. His face was now rid of its former softness.

"You're going to take me to my money. You're going to do it right now," De Olmos said.

Another man came and grabbed Beau and walked him over to the first SUV. The man shoved him in the back seat, pushed Beau over to the middle of the bench, and then hopped in himself. The other men went back to either this SUV or the other, while two other men got into Beau's truck just ahead. The SUVs followed these men in Beau's truck down the road and onto the ranch road leading to the ranch itself. The vehicles all pulled into the driveway and parked.

CHAPTER 14 – BACK IN THE WORLD

As Beau looked out the windshield he could see the barn out on the ranchland. Again he noticed at its first sight that the front of the barn looked like a face set to a yell. Through the lens of this vehicle, and in its present company, that face appeared all the more ominous, its yell some dark message that could now almost be heard with ear as well as soul. As Beau looked at this face and its great mouth he realized in the moment that only he saw its jaws open to receive them. Only he heard its song. Only he knew of what it carried in its belly.

The men forced Beau out and onto the driveway, where De Olmos and the others were waiting. De Olmos said not a word, but stood looking at him with expectation. Senior's trailer was parked on the side of the house in plain view no more than a hundred feet away. De Olmos had not so much as looked at the trailer.

Beau looked out onto the land at the barn. He gestured towards it with a shake of his head. "I got it in there."

De Olmos nodded. "Okay."

The man behind Beau pushed him forward from behind his shoulder, causing Beau to take several smaller steps to retain his balance. Beau looked back up to De Olmos. "We're going to need a flashlight."

De Olmos nodded to one of the other men who moved back to the SUV to fetch one.

"… And a bolt cutter," Beau said again.

De Olmos squinted at this.

"I got a set in the truck."

The group of men stood looking down at the cellar door

on the ground behind the barn. Beau was at the front of the group. As he stared at the padlock which clasped the door shut he remembered that his father had put that lock on the door. For good reason. A reason he was about to set aside. The men beside him spoke to one another in Spanish.

"Go on," De Olmos said.

"I need my keys."

A man standing by De Olmos stepped to Beau and jabbed the keys down into his open hand. Beau came forward to the door and knelt down. He found the small key and used it to turn the padlock open. He tossed the padlock on the ground and took hold of the door handle and swung it open as he stood up. Unlike the two times prior, he let the door swing free and come crashing down on the ground heavy, making a loud clang which reverberated like a gong.

Beau looked down into the dark. "You coming?"

De Olmos smiled. "Get my money."

Beau stared down into the dark for a moment longer. Beau then leaned back to the ground and retrieved the flashlight and bolt cutter. He turned on the flashlight and pointed it down into the dark.

As Beau began the first step down, De Olmos said – "Be mindful that all the things you love are still up here. If you come back up with anything but my money, I'll burn them all to a cinder. All of them. To a cinder and that's a promise."

"I'll get what's yours."

Beau walked the stairs to their bottom and looked into the dark ahead. The flashlight he used was not as powerful as the lantern that he had brought before. He could see the locker out at the cellar's edge only dimly. He stared at it for a moment thinking. Thinking about the tragedy already coiled about him and coiling further. If a thing deserved could be called a tragedy at all. A vision came to mind of a constrictor tangled around a rat, crushing its life out of it from its core until it all came pouring out its eyes and nose and ears and mouth and every other such place that such things could run from its center. Such pressure and pain as would make the life lived up to that point not worth its ending. He wondered if such a rat at that moment of breaking would trade its place to within a different constrictor's grasp, if only that snake would promise to devour the first when it was done. Beau looked back up the stairs to the several faces staring down at him from the world above. He believed that such rat would. At least the rat would die not as a victim only, but as something of a viper himself.

Beau walked to the locker directly with the light pointed at the areas where the slits and eyes would soon appear. Which they did. Beau came directly to the front of the locker door and looked into those eyes, ready to begin.

"There are men up there that aim to kill me and everything about me."

The man in the box looked into Beau's eyes, grasping at what was filling the contours of Beau's lot there before him.

"There's people that would pay for being parts in things that they had no intention to be part of. Only to be part in me," Beau said again.

"Maybe that alone justifies their payment."

"You want out of that box or not?"

"What does that have to do with it?"

"Because I'll let you out if you kill them."

The eyes of the man caught this statement something terrible. "You don't know what you're doing."

"If I let you out, these men are dead," Beau paused. "Tell me I'm wrong."

The man inside pondered the man without. Something of a tapping came from lower in the box. And then quiet. "You're wrong," the voice said.

The man's answer landed heavy. Beau grimaced. He ran his hand through his hair as a gambler might upon losing his last chance of a line of last chances, knowing that there were no more to be found in all of creation. Beau sat down on the dirt, as if he had no other choice but to do so.

"These men are dead," the voice continued. "Whether you let me out or not. If you don't, they'll kill you, and then they'll be down soon enough. They'll let me back into this world. And they'll die because of it."

Beau looked back up to the eyes, with the desperation and darkness in his own heart yet clinging to the darkness it hoped to ride through these men's skulls. And that darkness had confirmed its dark end. As he had hoped it would.

"But you're still wrong. Wrong more deeply," the man said. "There are many things worse than dying."

Beau stood up. He looked to those eyes again.

"As for your part in all this," the man began again. "It could end right now. You could be free. Even if you die."

Beau reached into his pocket and took out the keyset. Beau found the same small key, inserted the key into the padlock, and turned. The key turned through the frozen

138

time of inactivity stuck in the rotation of the lock jam. It creaked and popped with a sound unnatural of a grind. But it popped still. And was now open.

"No one has ever got away with anything," the man said in a quieter voice.

For the first time in this encounter, Beau felt the tremble of hesitation. A panic's choice giving way to exacting reality. The door had been opened. Maybe many doors, both seen and unseen, and this voice was all but back in the world. Beau took a step back as he pulled the door open inch by wretched inch. The heaviness of the door moved slow as he pulled it against the thickness of time that had settled into the hinges. Beau's heart hammered within his chest as he prepared for the sight of the thing. Like a child who has caught an awful spider beneath a cup who must build the courage to pull it back and look true at the creature within.

But he was no beast. In the gray of the light's beam stood a man. It seemed. His face made of the ancient and bronzed skin of those beautiful people native to these desert plains, with jet black hair that hung down behind his head into the dark of the locker. He appeared middle-aged, but with a youth and beauty and health about his face that was altogether evasive in definition and yet present and tangible. A man. Beau stepped back from him just as the man stepped forward and out of the locker.

The man stared Beau down. Intensity colored with danger and hunger and death. The man looked down to his own torso, which was wrapped in thick bands of black-iron chains over and over again. The man's clothes were but ribbons dangling from himself indiscernible as to their original form. Beau saw at the middle of the man's left side the vised clasp that held the chains taut. Beau lifted the bolt cutter in his left hand in inquiry to approach. The man stared back, his stillness his acquiescence. Beau stepped carefully and quietly, as if somehow he could not help but move in a manner like he was sneaking up on the man and the dark aura about him. As if something might be asleep yet in the dark with them that Beau wished not to awaken.

Beau had to take an arm of the cutter in each hand and could not figure what to do with the small flashlight. Beau saw nothing else around to rest it upon to shine the light on the task. At last Beau put the back of the flashlight in his mouth and bit down on its end to hold it fast. Beau pointed his face and the beam of the flashlight down at the clasp. He reached out with the bolt cutter trembling gently within his hands. The tremble and awkward nature of the flashlight held between his quickly tiring jaw caused him some short moments of trouble in grasping the clasp within the cutter's teeth. Beau took a second and let out a breath and then clamped the cutter true on the clasp. Beau looked once more up to the man's eyes with the flashlight shaking within his jaw's grip. The dark of the man's eyes stared back with some awful anticipation and the thought did cross Beau's mind that this breath in his lungs was the last that would ever be.

Beau squeezed the arms of the cutter together to the tension point and grunted between his breath as he applied further pressure through the impasse. Drool ran out of the right corner of his mouth which was bracketed open by the flashlight. A hollow clink sounded as the cutter snapped the clasp – with the release of this tension sending Beau off balance and shuffling sideways and falling to the dirt. The flashlight fell out of his mouth during the fall and Beau slapped the thing clear ten feet away with his flailing arm. As Beau hit the dirt he was already to bracing himself for some onset of pain. This fear set him to rolling into a ball and shutting his eyes and bringing his hands over his ears like a thing returning to infancy before its departure.

Beau laid like that on his side. For five seconds, clenching every muscle about him for that falling hammer. And then five seconds more. And then for some seconds more before he could stand it no longer and opened his eyes, expecting to see the man's eyes inches from his own and waiting for this moment.

But Beau saw no such thing. He saw nothing at all in the dark around him. He looked over to the flashlight on the dirt some ten feet away and shooting its beam sideways in another direction. The flashlight levitated upward quickly. The outline of the man was behind it, indiscernible beyond his contours. Click. And the light was off. And it was dark.

Beau laid his head back on the dirt, balled in this position, still with his hands over his ears. He did not close his eyes. And he waited now for the man to come and kill him as he knew that he would.

But again, nothing. No pain. No onset of the man's grip. No sound. Nothing. Beau remained still for some more moments as this all set in. Beau took his hands from his ears. He sat up in the dark and listened again. But he heard nothing more, save for his own breath. He looked to the only light in that space, which came from far on the other side of the cellar at the opening atop the flight of stairs.

Beau sat and stared over at that light a long while from his place on the dirt. A whole half-hour. He could not think of the first thing to do. He found himself thinking about Jonah down in the belly of the great fish. Down in the belly of some beast somewheres is where most all outlaws will find themselves eventually. Swallowed and digesting in dark places. Once the panic had worn out on Jonah, it must have been quiet. So quiet. Until he could at the last reflect on himself and his rebellion, since death's juices rejected the nourishment of him yet. As if the point of the whole narrative was to bring him to that place where he could do nothing but set out on such reflection. Reflect until the path before him was cleared. The path back out the mouth which had devoured him. And Beau stood up. And Beau walked to the stairs and looked up at the sky, hearing not a thing. And Beau walked up the stairs into the world once again.

Scattered about the earth around the cellar door were randomized articles of clothing and things formerly carried by the men. One boot here with the other twenty feet apart, a torn shirt with blood about it, a half a sock, a jean leg with no leg present. Lonely guns on the gravel, sunglasses, a wrist watch, hats, a clump of matted hair. The top of the gravel was caked with a dark substance for the entirety of twenty feet surrounding the scene. Beau knelt down and took a bit of this gravel between his fingers and rubbed them together until the blood smeared out over his touch with the gravel no longer holding together and falling to the earth from which it had come. There were no bodies, save

142

for one – De Olmos, lying alone and motionless twenty feet away.

Beau looked out and around the land for anything else, but all was empty, as if from a time removed entirely from the evidences of the act around him. Beau walked to De Olmos and stared down at him. One of De Olmos' eyes was wide open as if in surprise, while the other was half-shut and lethargic and emptied. His mouth was ajar and his teeth stained black with the blood he had coughed up in those moments, with the spray of such horrid coughs dried atop the rest of his face. De Olmos' throat was ripped open. Like a thick cloth torn. On his chest lay a small pile of golden trinkets of all kinds and wads of blood-stained cash of several hundred dollars in various denominations.

Beau studied the edges of the mess until he found the set of prints leaving the scene. One set only. A narrow boot. The set led out of the scene at a walking stride straight toward the fence at the edge of the land with the vast desert landscape sprawled out behind it. The desert stood wide and deep, like the face of some ocean's abyss, where a dark thing could sink to such a depth and to such a darkness as to negate the thought of a search at all. A thing gone.

Beau grabbed De Olmos by the ankles of his boots and dragged him across the mud back to the cellar door. The old man's legs were already setting to a lock. Beau dragged his frail body down the cellar stairs by his boots too, stair-by-stair, with the old man's head falling with a pound upon each of the planks. Beau dragged him to the back corner of the cellar and left him in the dark without thinking to look at him again.

Beau gathered up the scattered articles on the ground until his arms were full and took these things down and threw them atop and around the body of De Olmos. After several such trips, the ground around the cellar door was cleared except for the bloodied earth. Beau took a shovel from within the barn and dug and stirred up this mud with the dry earth underneath the best he could. The earth was still darkened to an off hue, but was not bloody to the touch any longer.

Beau opened up the side gate and drove his truck right up to the cellar door. Beau tried as he could not to look at what once had been Stills' face as he pushed the bloodied mass of his body off of the opened gate of the truck. The fat and bloated body met the ground with a heavy slap. All types of fluids continued to run from the man. Beau dragged Stills down the cellar stairs as well by his boots, but tried with some more effort not to bang what had been the man's head from stair to stair. Beau did not put Stills in the same corner with De Olmos and what was left of the others. Beau dragged him with much strain at this point to the other side of the cellar entirely. As Beau caught his breath in the dark, looking down at this poor figure, he knew that there were many who at this moment still thought that man a part of this world. Of their world. And Beau knew that once this piece was found to be missing, many such worlds would fold upon themselves and this hole. Beau thought what to say to him, as if something should be said. But he only shook his head at it all. At himself and what might be left of his own soul. What Stills was a part of now Beau did not know, but it was no longer this world, and the liability for such passage was his own.

Beau connected the hose to the nozzle at the side of the barn. It stretched just far enough to reach his truck. Beau opened up both doors of the cab and washed out the blood and matter and glass with as high a spray as the hose would allow. He kept on until the water running down off the seats no longer had any tint to it at all. Beau turned off the hose and looked over the interior of the truck again. He stared through the hole left in the windshield from the bullet that had run through Stills' head.

Beau drove the truck into the barn and parked it up against the back wall. He walked back to the door of the barn and closed and locked it. Beau walked across the land back toward the driveway where the two SUVs were still parked. Beau looked at them and thought on it.

Beau could think of no way to rid himself of them completely at the time. Beau tied the one to the other on their respective hitches with a tow strap from the garage. Beau put the rear vehicle into neutral and backed the front vehicle into it with a sure enough force to send both to a roll down the driveway. When the rear vehicle had rolled out past the middle of the road, Beau hit the brakes and braced himself as the rear vehicle jolted the first and dragged it several feet until the both of them came to a stop. Beau drove the vehicles a mile down the road and turned out onto the open mesa land. Beau drove another mile until the road could no longer be seen from the driver's mirror and he stopped. Beau detached the tow strap from the rear SUV and left it there in the desert and drove back to the ranch.

Beau leaned against the wall of the shower in his parents' bathroom as the warm water ran over him and carried the waste of the day from off of his flesh. Beau's hair was stuck together in clumps of some residue he could not decide upon and it took much time from washing before he could feel it all gone. The running of the water washed all of it down the drain eventually. What could be seen.

Beau picked out a pair of folded jeans and a white t-shirt from Senior's side of the closet. He found a pair of semi-worn work boots amidst other shoes in the closet as well. He put on this outfit and walked out of the room, avoiding a look at any of the mirrors around the room lest he catch a glimpse of the imposter walking in his father's clothes. Once downstairs, Beau crumpled his bloodied and soiled outfit into a trash bag. He walked out back and stuffed this trash bag down into the midst of the trash that filled the bin. The sun was all but down out on the horizon. Beau lost sight of the buried bag in the heap amidst the shadow and dark that poured in along top of it.

Beau drove the SUV back to town and within a couple of blocks away from the station. He parked the SUV in an alleyway where it would eventually be noticed and ticketed and then towed away. Beau wiped the steering wheel clean with a rag and then wiped all the handles the same. He looked the cab over to make sure he had left nothing behind. Beau left the vehicle unlocked and walked away.

Beau did not engage in conversation with anyone at the station, but only walked to Senior's office direct. Beau found the keys to Senior's department truck in the top drawer of the desk. He took the keys and walked back out of the station, again not engaging with anyone and not looking anyone in the face. He went to the back lot where the department vehicles were parked. He saw Senior's truck parked and waiting in the Sheriff's spot.

Susie and Jean were in the living room watching the news on the television when Beau walked into the house. Susie looked to him and stared for a moment recognizing his outfit being off.

"There's chicken and fixings on the stove for tacos," Susie said, still looking at him while turning down the volume a few clicks on the controller in her hand.

"Okay," Beau said, standing there.

"You hungry?"

Beau looked to his mother sitting a few feet to Susie's side. The glow from the changing colors of the television moved on her face. She kept on watching without paying much attention to him.

"Uh huh," Beau said.

Susie looked on at Beau, her eyes sizing up what she could from him. Beau stood by silent and let such inventory conclude. "Well go get you some."

In the middle of that night, Beau crept out of bed from beside her and snuck downstairs to the kitchen as quiet as he could. Beau turned on the light in the kitchen and sat down at the table and laid out the address book. Beau found Reverend's number. Beau dialed the number on the pad of the phone hanging on the wall. As it rang, he turned off the light switch at the side of the phone and the kitchen went dark. The phone rang four times and then Beau hung it up.

Beau walked quietly up the stairs and eased himself back into bed. When he looked at Susie, she was staring at him awake. Beau stared back in the quiet for some moments and then closed his eyes. The last thing he heard

147

before falling off to sleep was the whispers of her praying and he imagined her still looking on.

- Beau

My Grandad was a traveling evangelist preacher from West Texas. Midland. He was tough the way people from West Texas are. He spoke like you would have thought the prophets spoke, with a voice deep and slow and resonant. I heard him tell Dad one time that he thought the Lord had used him to bring ten thousand souls to the kingdom. That such was proof that the Lord could use any old fool to effect His will. Truth is, he said, the Lord could raise up children for Abraham from the stones if he chose to, as the Book says. Not a doubt in his mind.

Grandad and Grandma, tired of his traveling, eventually settled on a small ranch south of Albuquerque near Bosque Farms, down a quarter mile from the banks of the Rio Grande. Sam and I would go up there and stay for a whole month each summer, with nothing to do but run loose around the brush and trees up and down that muddy river valley. At nights, Grandad would tell us stories from the older testament, which he knew by heart such that he would animate them vivid before us with his voices, always waving his hands about. Telling us about the kings and the judges. And how wicked it was for the people to ask God for a king. He loved talking about King David. How the king, though anointed, and with a heart for the Lord unique among men, was flawed deep, such that many died for Bathsheba, and later for his failure to judge the wrong under his own roof. Many died for it, even his own boys, one as a babe, and the other, Absalom, was snatched up by an oak tree and caught by the head out in the woods of Ephraim until his enemies come by and spit him like a pig. Grandad's telling of such stories from the Book were always alive, and most always themed with sin and blood.

Grandma passed in the night while we were up there one summer. It was only a handful of months before Sam himself would meet the Lord. I heard an awful noise before the sun was up, like a calf in distress, calling out in pain somewheres to its momma. It was Grandad, toughest man I have ever known, bawling without any type of restraint from inside his bedroom. Wailing is a word that fits. The door was shut. He only yelled out to me in composing himself that I was to go back to bed. Some men came and got Grandma later that morning and took her away.

Grandad went walking outside after lunch. I found him standing all by himself, looking out at the row of cottonwoods which lined this side of the river. Standing there with his hands in the pockets of his jeans, he looked to me a man at once alone and small in the world about him. I walked up to him and stood beside him, looking out with him at the scene. I said, "Grandad, was Grandma scared of dying?" "I don't know son. Probably some." I asked again, "Are you scared of dying?" He took in a breath and let it out. "I wasn't before. But I guess I never truly saw it. Strange. I'm scared as could be."

The dogs were barking. Barking and howling like they were on fire. It awoke Abigail with a gasp. She sat up in bed and listened to the roaring of the hounds hold steady for some thirty seconds. "What they got into out there?"

she said into the dark of the room with no one to hear. One of the dogs set to snarling and snapping between its yells as if it was lurching at something. "The hell you got into back there?" Abigail rose from bed and secured the nightgown around her.

Abigail walked downstairs to the sliding glass door at the side of the kitchen. She looked out through the glass at the dog-run all in the dark. The hounds had only intensified their cries. Abigail turned on the porch light. The two hounds were frantic behind the fence. Pacing the boundary, showing their teeth, and snarling out at the dark.

Abigail unlocked the door and opened it a foot. "Hey! What's going on out there!"

The dogs paid the woman no mind and continued on yelling and pacing about.

"Hey! What's gotten' into the both of you! I mean it!"

The male rose up on his hind legs and leaned up against the fence and let out a howl at the night that came from the deepest parts of its throat. It was unlike any sound Abigail had ever heard a dog make and it sent a chill down her neck. Abigail opened the door more and walked out a few steps onto the porch. She looked around the yard that was made visible by the porch light and saw nothing. The dark at the edges of the yard was thick.

Abigail walked towards the fence while the hounds kept at it, looking past her into the dark and shouting their warnings and anger at the unseen. The look of terror in the male's eyes caused Abigail to look back over her shoulder twice during this short walk, but still there was nothing to be seen or heard.

Abigail made it to the fence directly in front of the

middle point of the hounds' pacing. "Hey there! Hey!" she said to them in a stern voice while the hounds snapped and cried back towards the dark, still not looking at her. "Hey! Hey! Hey!" she yelled. The hounds did not calm. "Brutus!" she shouted at the tops of her lungs at the male. "Brutus! Stop!"

And in an instant they did. The both of them drew quiet. They were still looking past Abigail out to some spot behind her. The female laid down on the ground and rested her muzzle on the dirt, looking downward. The male sat back on his rear at full attention. His eyes were yet strained with some strong feeling.

Abigail turned to see what the male was staring at once again and now saw the dark outline of a man standing at the edge of the lit porch. His face was covered by the dark. The sight of it took her breath from her. He was not moving. Just looking on at her, still as could be. She secured the nightgown around her as terrible images filled her head of what might happen to her in the next moments of her life.

The figure took steps forward into the light and stopped. He was a Native American man with long hair pulled back behind his shoulders. He looked at Abigail with empathy in his eyes, as if sorry for what he was about to do. Several moments passed between the two of them as he stared at her with this look upon his face.

The fear was a pain that filled up her stomach. She could feel him about to move and could take it no more. He was too close to the door. She ran off into the dark of the desert without looking back.

Each step was fresh with pain as the barbs of the desert

floor pierced her bare feet. She was crying. She moaned and staggered every few steps from this pain. But she did not stop. She could hear nothing coming after her, which she knew was not true, and only kept the edge of the terror sharp upon her.

She ran for what must have been ten whole minutes before she turned to look back for the first time. She was still running, but saw nothing behind her in the night. She kept on. Between bush, through cacti, over a washed out bed of run off, down a long stretch of slope, and up the other side. The chilled air burned down deep in her lungs. When she reached the top of this hill, she fell to her knees. She sucked in the air between her cries. The lacerations all underneath her feet throbbed while the blood ran down and beneath her toes. She fell onto her side and cried. She reached down and clutched her feet, feeling them sopped with wetness. It was quiet all around her.

A snap sounded in the desert somewhere back from where she had come. Her head shot up. She looked but could see nothing. She listened for several moments, but could hear nothing more.

She put the palms of her hands flat onto the gravel and pushed herself back up onto all fours. She took in several breaths and then pushed herself up more, eventually bringing one of her feet up to standing. There was the sharp sting from the earth pressing up into the tears under her foot. She brought her other foot up with similar pain and pushed on her knees with both hands until she was standing again.

She looked back over the desert land she had crossed and saw her house out in the short distance, alone on the desert landscape, except for the twinkling of other house lights some miles more. The moon was alone in the sky. It shone down on the scene, which appeared serene and quiet to her in that moment. Her breath slowed gradually as she looked out upon it all. And for a moment, she felt something of a calm. Not as if she had escaped. But that this scene, this world, was ancient, and would be here always.

A sound something like a breeze came from out towards her house. It was faint at first, but grew steadily by the moment. It grew and grew until it was a wind, a sound of no particular origin, a rush, a force in the air. It grew until it was loud. And then as it was close, it broke into the night around her, and faded until it was quiet again.

She heard the voice of a man, as if almost in her ear, say something in a soothing tone that she could not make out. Then all she saw was black.

***

Harold snapped awake from the scream of his wife just before he felt her leap over to his side within the bed and clutch his arm. He looked up and around the room, in shock from his awakening. He looked all around, coming to, though nothing caught his eye. He looked to his wife's face, she was looking toward the reading chair at the corner of their room. Someone was sitting in it. Looking at them.

Harold reached his arm out to the side of the bed toward the nightstand and turned the knob on a small lamp. This lamp threw a dim light upon the room and the intruder. It was a man with long, dark hair, and a soft expression upon his face. The man looked upon them without much change upon his face, as if his presence was a casual thing.

Margaret said Harold's name out loud in a whisper. The couple looked on at the man, and he looked on at them, as if no one had to move in the situation.

"What do you want?" Harold asked the man.

The man did not respond.

"I, I got some money in my desk. In the office there down the hall."

The man still looked at them with soft eyes.

"Mister, we don't have much," Harold said.

The man only continued to look on. Content. As if the act of looking at them was what he had come for. The man stood up slowly. He walked the five or six steps to the foot of the bed with the same gentle face. He stopped at the foot of the bed and looked down upon them. Margaret's grip upon Harold's arm tightened. Harold looked up at the man, the two of them meeting eyes for a last moment between them.

***

Tom drove his truck down the dark country road as blues music played over the radio. He tapped the steering wheel as he rode along. The truck shifted and swayed from the dirt road's imperfections.

Tom caught movement at the dark edge of the road just ahead from the corner of his eye. Something walked out of the black of the desert and began crossing over the road. Tom screamed out as he dropped his foot down on the brake and brought his other hand back up to the steering wheel for the sudden stop. The truck shook violently as the tires tried desperately to catch a grip of the gravel road top. The figure just out in front continued to walk across the road, with its head yet looking straight ahead as if it did not notice or care about what seemed to be an imminent collision.

The figure walked just past the path of the skidding truck as it screeched by at the end of its stop. The figure did not look back at the truck, but just kept walking until it had disappeared into the dark of the desert at the other side of the road.

The truck at last stopped. Tom sat still in the truck, catching his breath as the engine idled softly. "Goddamn," he said to himself in the quiet. It was strange how quiet everything had become, though his heart pounded still.

A tap came at the window. A man was looking in at him. A Native American man with long hair hanging free. Tom looked up at him for a moment, still catching up to what had happened. The man knocked again with the backs of his knuckles.

Tom held his left hand up. "Hold on." With his other hand, Tom reached down underneath the seat and felt around until he got hold of his pistol. Tom took hold of it in his hand. He pushed out the safety with his thumb and brought the pistol out from underneath the seat to behind his leg so as to keep it hidden. The man knocked again.

"Okay," Tom said again.

Tom rolled the window down manually with his left hand several inches so he could hear the man. "What the hell you doing out here?" Tom asked. "You in some kind of trouble?"

The man's fist burst through the window faster than Tom's eyes could follow and latched onto the center of Tom's throat. The man's grip was like a vise. Tom could not breathe, he could not swallow. The arteries in his neck were blocked. Stars appeared before his eyes within seconds. He felt the life leaving him immediately.

Tom's left hand had been grabbing at the man's hand around his throat. The strength of this man was far beyond him. The gun had fallen out of Tom's other hand. Tom reached with his right arm as far as he could and grasped about the floor with his fingertips. He felt it. Tom used what life he had to lower his body within the man's grip just enough to grab the gun. Tom raised it up to the man's head.

But the man's free hand appeared and gripped the barrel of the pistol before it could be leveled at his head. Tom was at the edge of losing consciousness and did not have the strength left to pull the trigger anyhow. Tom was blacking out, but he did believe that he saw the barrel of the gun squish as putty in the man's hands before Tom felt a great tug from the man at his throat.

Tom was pulled out of the window and dropped onto the road. Air and blood began to run once again through his throat, though Tom knew it crushed. Tom felt another strong tug on his arm. The night sky moved above him as the man drug him across the road and out into the desert.

- Beau

When I was a small boy, my brother Sam would take me down to the back fence at night sometimes to look out into the dark of the country. We would go way down on the edge of our land, far from the house, back where the mesa lands began again. If you didn't know any better, you would have thought you were in the middle of that desert with nothing for miles and miles. I don't think I have ever since been to a place so dark and so quiet. At least in my own mind.

We would bring the pellet guns that Dad had given us and sit and look out into the dark listening. Some nights we heard the coyotes, yippin' and bawlin' at each other as they chased down their meals in the black. Some other times we caught the shrill of a desert cat out on the plain, screeching out at something that had spooked it. Many times we weren't sure what we heard, calls from unknown beasts running about behind their dark curtain, sometimes far, sometimes close. I do recall being afraid. But not of such things. My strongest recollections come from those times when we heard nothing at all. When the dark was still all around us. When my mind would wander. I would get this shudder down deep in my gut. I know you have felt something like it at some point in your life. That feeling like there was something there. Like every bit of my being was telling me there was something out there in all that dark and all that quiet. Something to be afraid of.

One night when Grandad and Grandma were down

visiting, we brought Grandad out there with us. And after some time spent looking out upon the dark of that place, he began to tell us the story of the fall of Adam. Not like he had before, but with detail and emphasis like a horror story. The serpent, the fruit, the whispers, the hiding from the Lord Himself in the garden as He walked through in the cool of the day, all sinister as could be. And though the Lord tended to them, He drove them out of that place, and set there mighty angels and a flaming sword which turns every which way, so that no one may return. And there came the curse, from which each man has returned to dust ever since. Except the One.

That scared feeling that comes natural in a dark place has ever since impressed upon me a distinct meaning. As it must have to Grandad to elicit the story in that moment. I've thought a lot about it. Though the feeling itself is without tangible explanation, by design I think, I do not feel it insignificant. The fact it can be perceived, and by all, speaks of some importance which should give you pause. Like an echo left in the air of this world that's purpose is to remind the observer that there is something to be feared. And though its exact meaning can be argued by each their own interpreter, the picture that has settled in my mind within such feeling ever since has been that of Adam's fall. A reverberation's evidence, of both the event, and scale of its consequences. The noise of the thing left in the air. A reminder. That there is no such thing as indifference.

Beau heard Susie calling his name in his sleep. Then he heard it again. Then he heard it again more loudly and awoke.

"Get up," Susie said. "Beau, get up."

Beau lifted his head up from his pillow and looked to her.

"There's a man sitting on the porch."

"What?"

"Beau, there's a man on the porch."

"Who is?"

"I don't know. I've never seen him before."

"What's he doing?"

"I told you. Sitting."

Beau leaned up and rubbed out his eyes.

"What did he say to you?"

"I didn't say anything to him."

Beau got out of bed and picked up jeans from off the floor and put them on. He could not see a shirt around. He wrapped a blanket from the bed around him and walked downstairs. Susie followed behind him until they reached the front door.

Beau unlocked the door and opened it enough to look out through the screen door and onto the porch beside the doorway. It was him. The man sat on the bench looking out over the desert stretching across the earth to the horizon, which was filling with pink and orange from the sun beginning to rise back into the world. He was sitting still. His face sober. He did not look over.

"Who is he?" Susie whispered behind him.

Beau stood quiet, still looking.

"Do you know him?" she asked again.

"Yes."

"You want me to call the office?"

"Don't call anyone."

"Why didn't you bring the pistol down?"

Beau looked back to her for the first time since being downstairs. He didn't say anything.

Beau pushed the screen door open and stepped out onto the porch. Beau stood there looking at the man. The man was wearing jeans with cowboy boots on his feet. He had a heavy cowhide jacket on. His hair was pulled back. The man did not react to him, but just kept looking out to the horizon.

"This is my home," Beau said.

The man did not respond. He kept looking out as if he had not heard.

"I let you go," Beau said again.

"Is that what you did?"

A chill blew in off the desert. Beau pulled the blanket tighter around himself. "What do you want?"

The man sat quiet on that question. "What do you think I am?" the man asked, not having looked away from the sunrise.

"I don't know," Beau said. "I don't know what you are."

"You afraid?"

"I saw what you did."

"What we did."

"What business we had is over."

The man turned his eyes slowly to Beau. "What we have between us is all you have left." The man let this stare set for a moment. He then looked back out to the horizon. "You really surprised I'm here?"

Beau did not respond.

"That's the problem right there, isn't it? With all of it?" the man took in a deep breath of the morning air, as if such breath was special and satisfying.

"You don't think that you're as rotten as them, do you?" the man said again.

"I'm not the same as them."

"Maybe you're worse. You think you can get away with how you are."

"Don't hurt her," Beau said. "You don't have cause to hurt her. She's not a part of this."

"She's a part of you."

The breeze made a soft whistle on the porch.

"I'm going down south of here. Out to all those canyons and mesas. Mesas like small mountains."

It was quiet again.

"You know where this is?"

"Don't hurt her."

The man took in another deep, intentional breath, and let it out through his nostrils. "You're going to meet me out there tonight. You're going to look me in my eyes and admit what you are. And you're going to throw yourself off into the dark of that place."

It was quiet again, save for the breeze.

"That's how it'll be. You do that, nobody else will get hurt."

The man rose from the bench, still staring out at the sunrise. He looked over to Beau. "It's a tragedy that all the world is like you." The man put his hands in the pockets of his jacket and walked down the steps of the porch.

"How do I find you?" Beau asked.

162

The man continued walking, "you just keep on. We'll find each other."

The man walked down the driveway on his way to the road. Beau watched him go. The man made it to the road, crossed over, and walked out into the desert land. He walked a slow and straight path over the brush, rock, and cacti. A thing pulled back out to the wild. With a path before him that man cannot see, though it is there. Like the beasts of the desert that have lived on those plains for millennia, who have never been lost. And as he became smaller in the distance, so too did the fear in Beau's heart, for even this thing looked small in the world around him.

Susie was standing behind the screen door, watching everything. "What have you done?"

"I don't know where to begin."

"Did you hurt somebody? Beau. Did you hurt somebody?"

Beau nodded his head. Beau looked to her, and though it was hard, he looked to her eyes. She measured him there, as she could.

"Who is he?" she asked.

Beau shook his head. "I don't know."

She saw something behind him that took her eyes from him. Beau looked back. Out distant on the road there was a flashing of blue and red. Susie opened the screen door and stepped out onto the porch. She walked past him. Beau stepped forward and the both of them watched the squad car draw closer. When it was within a hundred yards of the driveway, its lights turned off.

The squad car pulled into the driveway and rolled to a stop. A female deputy was at the wheel by herself. She looked on them with a sadness. She got out of the car and took off her uniform hat and held it down at her hip. She came to the porch.

"Something awful's happened. Coleman's folks. I thought I better come out myself."

The sheets of their bed were soaked in blood. It was a lot of blood. Blood on the ground by the bed as well. There was no sign of them. There were boot prints walking away from the bedroom down the hall, but they gradually ran out before the end of the hallway. The rest of the house was in order. All the doors. All the windows. And though the scene did not tell the whole story, all who saw it knew that they were gone.

Beau stood several feet back from the bed, looking over it. His stomach hurt and he thought he would be sick. Two of the deputies were taking pictures and measurements, gathering things from off the ground. Beau knew what had happened here. Who was responsible. Beau knew that no one else here would ever know that, which was as lonely a feeling as he could remember. It made his stomach hurt all the more. He could look at it no more and left the room.

Coleman sat at the kitchen table. He was not wearing his uniform. He had on a black t-shirt and jeans, though he had on his deputy hat. His face was pale. He stared at an arrangement of plastic fruit in a bowl at the center of the table, though he was really looking to some far off place.

Beau walked to the other side of the table and sat down in the chair. He took off his hat and placed it on the table. He did not want to lie to Coleman. Anything he might have said would have been a lie, so he sat quiet and let Coleman be quiet. It was silent between them a while.

"I had a dream about my dad last night," Coleman said. "Your daddy was there too. They were both younger men, sitting on chairs out on the porch together, like from when they would take us fly fishing, and we would sit out on the porch at nightfall and listen to their stories. Watching them smoke their pipes. He looked at me. Kept on looking at me. He was thinking. Like he was weighing the man I was to become."

Coleman paused for a moment, as if he were seeing it all again. "And then I woke up. And I was lying there."

Coleman drew quiet on that. Still looking at that bowl of fruit. They both stayed quiet for a minute or so.

"Why would anyone hurt them?" Coleman asked.

Beau just looked at him. He knew that Coleman did not expect an answer. There was none. The two of them sat in the quiet a while longer.

A woman's voice came in over Beau's dispatch radio, "Sheriff? You there Sheriff?"

"Yeah," Beau said into the radio.

"We got a call a minute ago from Will Remey. Said he was out by Abigail Taylor's place and that she's gone. Said he thinks she's missing."

"Why?"

"Said when he got there he found the porch door open and her not in the house. Said he was to come by at eight to pick up the dogs to go hunting with him. He waited for an hour and she never did show up."

"He say anything else?"

"No sir."

"Tell him I'll be by."

Coleman insisted upon coming. Beau did not oppose

165

the man.

When they arrived at Abigail's house, they found Will sitting on the porch steps. Beau put the truck in park and looked on at Will. He could tell at first sight the man was scared.

When Beau and Coleman walked up to Will, before they could say anything, he started, "Beau I know something's happened to her."

"Hold on. Hold on."

"I came over and she was gone. We were supposed to meet first thing. Porch door was clear open. She wasn't in the house, I couldn't find her anywhere about."

"Why were you two meeting so early? Rose said something about you coming to get the dogs."

Will shook his head. "That wasn't it. I told Rose that because Abigail hadn't wanted the word out. We're involved. I was picking her and the dogs up, we were going to camp for a few days in the Weminuche. That's Silverton, past Durango."

Beau looked around at the scene before him. He noticed the dog-run at the side of the house. Coleman and Will followed. Beau found the dogs laying on the ground despondent. The male laid flat with his muzzle on the dirt. He looked up to Beau, but did not bother to pick his head up. Beau gave him a short whistle. The male did raise his head some and looked at Beau. He then dropped it back to the dirt.

Beau looked to the side of the yard and the desert beyond. He walked out to the yard's edge, looking out over that sprawling space in the quiet. Will and Coleman stood by in the yard. There was an imposing front of clouds mounting out at the horizon's edge. The day had grown colder before it.

"Is that her truck in the driveway?" Beau asked.

Will responded, "Yeah, next to mine there."

Beau continued to look out over the desert, thinking. Beau got his dispatch radio in his hand and pushed the call button. "Rose? Rose?"

"I'm here."

"What's the name of that fella at the Trooper's office up in Albuquerque that came by a few months back trying to get us to get one of them drug dogs. The fella that trains them up there?"

"I don't know his name. I'd have to check the calendar."

"Can you look him up and give him a call?"

"What you want me to tell him?"

"Ask him if he wouldn't mind getting a hold of some of them missing person dogs and sending a trooper down here."

"This for the Colemans?"

Beau was quiet for a moment. "Might be more than that."

"Okay."

"Rose?"

"Yes Sheriff."

"Call him now please. Thank you."

"Yes Sheriff."

Beau held the radio in his hand for a moment longer as if he was going to say something else.

"Sheriff?" the voice on the radio said again.

"Yes."

"Wendy's flagging me down. Says she wants to talk to you. Says she's got a call."

"Sheriff?" said another woman's voice.

"Yes Ms. Wendy."

"Sheriff we got another call that they found Tom Swanson's truck, that's Ned's boy that works down at the plant, they found his truck out not far from his house. They found it in park and still running right there in the middle of the road. Driver's side window was all smashed to bits. His pistol was laying out in the road too."

Beau and Coleman found the scene just as she had described it. There was another truck and two cars parked out near the subject truck. Passersby that had stopped. They were huddled all together by the side of one such car. They looked at Beau and Coleman with glares knowing that this was the site of some man's death. The man that was standing there kept looking at the pistol, which was half crushed at its barrel and just lying there in the middle of the road by the glass.

Beau and Coleman looked over the truck, but learned nothing new. Beau walked to the edge of the road and looked out again at the desert. The storm had grown all the more out on the plains. The world continued to become a colder place before it. Coleman walked over to his side to see what he was seeing. The desert was quiet.

"What has hell brought us?" Coleman asked.

"Hell ain't got a part in it."

The two kept on looking out over the plains. The beargrass swayed gently towards them with the breeze, the outer touch of the force of the storm beyond.

"I want you to come somewhere with me tonight,"

Beau started. "You know there ain't been but a few times in our lives that I've just asked you trust me. I want you to come with me tonight. I want to show you something."

Coleman looked at him, his face not revealing his thoughts. He turned and began walking back towards Beau's truck.

When Beau drove up to his parent's ranch house, his mother's car was in the driveway. He pulled in behind it and put the truck in park, though he did not turn off the engine yet. He sat and thought as the engine idled. Not sure if he still wanted to go in. Beau turned the truck off and got out.

When he came through the front door, he hollered out, "Momma!" She was not in the sitting room. "Momma!" he yelled again, "it's me!" It was quiet throughout the house.

Her voice came from somewhere upstairs, "Son?"

"Yeah Momma!" he shouted back.

"I'll be down!"

"You all right up there!"

"I'm fine!"

Beau walked to the back living room where Senior kept his large standing gun safe. Beau knelt down to the dial and turned in the combination until it clicked open. Beau reached in and got out Senior's long-range rifle. He looked it over. He found the scope in one of the safe drawers and took it out and attached it to the top of the rifle. Beau pointed the gun out the kitchen window and looked out through the scope into the desert. He brought the gun back down by his side. The soft-case for the gun was in the safe and he grabbed that too, along with a box of rounds. Beau

169

walked to the kitchen and laid out the case on the kitchen table and secured the rifle within it. He stuffed the pouch inside the case full with two dozen rounds and zipped the case back up.

Beau walked back to the front door and listened for his mother. He could not hear her moving. He stood there listening for a moment in the quiet. He then turned and looked over the sitting room, with most all furniture that had been there since he was a boy. Pictures too. He looked it all over and felt something like gratitude that there were such memories attached to the room. He then thought how he was going to miss everything. He then thought over whether the dead were capable of such a feeling. He turned and opened the front door quietly so as to not alert her that he was leaving. He closed the door quietly behind him too.

Beau walked down the front steps and began towards his truck in the driveway. A window opened upstairs above the front door and his momma's voice came through. "Hey! Where you think you're going?"

Beau looked to her in the window with the long rifle case slung over his shoulder. He shrugged his shoulders at her.

"You keep yourself right there, you hear, I'm coming down." She disappeared from the window.

Beau continued to the truck and opened it. He laid the rifle bag out on the back seat bench and shut the door to the truck before he heard the front door open.

She came out and stood on the porch, drying her hands with a towel. "Where you rushing off to? You don't have time for your mom?"

Beau walked on back to the bottom of the porch stairs

and looked up at her. He felt as if he wore the presence of the men stashed down in the cellar of the barn out back, and all of their blood about the yard, like a stain on himself. He wondered if such things were clear to her yet, or at least the feeling of such things. He knew he could not lie to her, and did not want to, though him standing there quiet was deceitful in its own right.

"I was just stopping by."

"Is that one of daddy's guns you got there?"

"Yes ma'am."

She looked at his face for a moment, seeing what it might reveal to her. "Well, they're all yours anyhow. You can come get em' all when you like."

He nodded and looked out sideways towards the yard. Not wanting to look to her eyes for too long. She kept quiet as if he might say something else.

"What are you doing here Momma? Don't you think it's better to stay with us for a while?"

Her expression showed she caught the deflection. "No son. This is my home. I'm meant to be home now."

"You want me to run you over something to eat?"

She sighed. "You don't have to tell me what's going on. You're a man. But you don't leave her in the dark anymore, you hear? She don't deserve that."

Beau looked to the ground.

"I don't have to tell you what kind of woman she is."

Beau kept quiet.

"Whatever you're into, I've raised you to do the right thing by it. You know what to do."

"Yes ma'am." He could not bring himself to look at her yet.

171

"You're looking shameful son."

"Yes ma'am."

"Whatever it is, it ain't complicated, not as you might think you have to make it."

Beau kept on looking down at the dirt.

"This ain't some kind of violence, is it? On account of daddy?"

Beau at last looked back up to her. "No."

"He was not a violent man. He wouldn't want violence."

"I know Momma."

She looked at his face deep. "I never raised you to be perfect Beau. No one is. No one can be. That cursed nature is still a part of us all. But I raised you to know how to handle when that nature comes out, didn't I?"

"You did."

"There ain't two ways to it. Repentance. If there's consequences, you be a man about them. But you don't go on and think you can force things right some other way. Never was a man that could. That's vanity. And many have gone to the grave for it."

Beau looked at her softly. He walked up the stairs and hugged her tight. He kept on hugging her for a moment. She hugged him back tight as she could. When he released her, he saw true concern upon her face. He took her face within his hands and kissed her forehead.

Beau turned and walked back down the stairs and then to the truck. He did not look back. He backed out the driveway, seeing her form in his periphery up on the porch. Watching him go. It was not a thing he could look at, and when he reached the road, he drove off without looking

172

back either.

- Beau

The next fall after Sam had passed, Grandad came down and picked me up and took me back up to Albuquerque to go to the state fair. I had been acting out. Struggling with it all. With the reality of the thing day by day proving itself something that would never be undone.

He took me to the fair three straight nights. We watched the cowboys riding those massive bulls, which were like monsters unreal to me raging out at all the world around them. We did see one poor fella that was thrown up in the air flailing like a child's doll before crashing to the earth and being trampled beneath the beast. We walked all the lanes of livestock. Seeing hogs as big as cars. And each night, we ate chili until our tongues were numb and our bellies full. Washed it all down with root beer. We rode every ride they had clear to midnight.

I was mostly respectful to Grandad during this time. I was old enough to appreciate what he was doing for me. Looking out for me as he was. There was an anger to me though that was not possible for a boy to put away entirely, not for long anyhow. On that last night we were at the fair, what I remember is that I walked out ahead of Grandad a ways by myself. When he pointed this out, I said something harsh to him, though I can't remember what it was now. After that, he just let me walk as I was, with him following some ways behind.

After a while, I looked back and could not find him. And in a moment I felt all the gravity of what it meant to be alone. All those lights and faces and sounds whirled about below the dark of the night sky. The abrupt grasp of such fear set me immediately to tears and me shouting out for Grandad, with people passing by looking at me like a thing peculiar and repulsive.

I finally saw him a distance back leaning against a booth and watching me. I was on a sprint to him the next moment and ran all the ways to him and crashed into him and hugged him tight. He said nothing as I cried, but only patted the middle of my back. When I had regained my breath, I asked him why he had left me.

"Left you?" he asked. "No." He brought me back in and hugged me for some more moments.

Grandad then knelt down so that his eyes could be on my level. He spoke softly, with his hands atop my shoulders. "There have been times in my life when I was set on walking away from the Lord. When I was angry. When I thought walking away was something like being free. And there have been times, when after some efforts, it did appear like He had let me. And at once, when I found myself alone, and felt something of the danger of what that meant, each time I have run back and found Him waiting. And I'm telling you it was grace that He let me walk to that place where I could feel such fear. Look, how many times have I told you that the fear of the Lord is the start of understanding? That proverb."

"A bunch."

"That means a right fear of who God is of course, because if that's missed, then all is missed. But the other side of that same coin is a fear of ourselves. Of that bent in our hearts to walk away from Him. Of being without Him,

175

the God of all the universe. Because a right understanding of the world is an understanding that there is nothing more terrifying than being apart from Him. It ain't freedom, is it? It's just being alone."

Susie was sitting on the bench of the front porch waiting for Beau when he came driving up the driveway. When the truck came to a stop, she rose from the bench and came to the front of the porch. Beau got out of the truck and looked at her for a moment before he closed the door. He left the rifle in the back.

Beau walked to the base of the porch steps and stopped there, looking up at her. He had never seen her face so tired. It put a pain to his heart. "After everything was done out on the highway," he began, "I found a sack full of money in the back of the car."

She looked down at him and let a quiet sit.

"I stole half of that money and locked it up in the trailer. Took it."

She took in a deep breath and exhaled it in receipt.

"That old man at the funeral, the one you were asking about, that was his money. He was a drug runner. Or something like it."

She looked upwards for a moment. She nodded, understanding the story from there.

"He told me if I gave it back. If I gave it back, he wouldn't hurt any of us." Beau shook his head and looked out to the side. "He would've killed us. That was his boy I put down out on the highway."

Beau took off his cowboy hat and held it down by his side. "That man you saw here this morning. I don't know who he is. I don't know how he came to be here. When Dad was about to pass, he told me he had someone locked away down in the cellar. Told me he was not a man at all."

"You let him go?" she asked.

"I did."

"'Cause you thought it would fix things? What else you had done?"

"Yes."

"Why?" she asked, shaking her head as if such was an obvious thing.

Beau shook his head too. "I can't say that I really know. I guess I thought I didn't know what he would turn out to be. But that's probably not true either."

"I haven't ever known you to be a coward."

Beau nodded.

"Or a liar."

Beau nodded again.

"How many?" she asked.

"How many what?"

"People?"

"Dozen, at least. I didn't know he would –"

"That's on us Beau."

"You don't have a part in it."

She shook her head again.

"They were the worst kind of men Susie, I didn't intend for –"

"You don't get it. How could you not get it? We aren't separate in anything. Ever."

Beau walked up the stairs to her. She took a step back at first to put more distance between them.

"This isn't you. It just ain't," she said.

"I've done all of it. It doesn't matter who I am."

"What are we going to do?"

"You heard him."

She shook her head thinking about what she had heard.

"There's no other way."

She closed her eyes, continuing to shake her head, as if at a fool. Beau stepped forward and put his arms around her and pulled her into himself. She now began crying. He held her and let her cry. After some moments she stopped any resistance to him and let her face sink into his chest. She sobbed into his chest. Crying about it all.

"I can kill this man."

With her head still in his chest, she said, "you're already gone."

Beau sat at the kitchen table watching her fix up a pot of chili. He kept silent as he watched her go about the kitchen fixing everything. She was beautiful to him. And though she was right there in front of him, she was far. Like a feeling. Like a memory of something playing out before him. Something like missing her.

They ate the chili sitting side by side at the table. It remained quiet, and the air something heavy, but they were together. Beau saw a tremble in her hand as she rested it on the table beside him. He reached out and took hold of it in his own hand, making it still.

When they were finished, they went to the living room and laid out on the couch. It was dark outside now and dark in the house. The living room was dimly lit by a soft lamp at the side of the room. Susie curled up beside him and rested her head upon his chest. He held her and rubbed her arm and shoulder over the blanket she wore. They remained quiet. Her eyes were closed. Beau stared out the window to the dark of the world which waited. Surrounding them there. He continued to rub her arm and looked out upon it.

The antique grandfather clock from out in the hallway ticked away in this quiet with its dull clacks upon the seconds. Though Beau rarely noticed such rhythm, it was amplified to him in this moment. And as he stared out at that dark, such rhythm became its heartbeat. Delicate and easy. But alive. And waiting. Beau understood in that moment that the character of the world around a person, what he saw, what he perceived, was but what he projected from within himself. That the matter of the world around him was ancient, and unchanging, as it always had been. But its energy, its character, was alive and always changing with what he filled it with. To some that night, the world was a calm thing within which they and their families resided, as parts in a home. But to men like him, this same world was a carnivore, hidden in its dark which it wrapped all about, lying in wait, with no rest, and with the quiet and calm its deception song.

The grandfather clock clanged, breaking this quiet. Susie's eyes opened. The clock clanged seven times. When the clangs stopped, they hung in the air. Susie leaned up and back and looked at him with all the fear in her heart rising to her face and crooking the sides of her mouth downward. Beau pulled her back into himself and held her tight as he could.

Beau turned on the outside light, opened the front door, and stepped out onto the porch. He was dressed in the thick camouflaged suit that he had worn for the past several years when hunting with his father in the cold. The light from the bulb beside him stretched out some twenty feet into the yard and illuminated the large clumps of snow that were falling. It was already sticking as a blanket on the earth. Beau's breath appeared before him in the light. Beau took off his cowboy hat and put on the black beanie from the pocket of his jacket and put the cowboy hat back on. He walked out to the edge of the porch. There was no wind to be heard. The giant flakes fell straight and quick in their waves. Poured out heavy and steady and placid. It was going to be a hell of a storm.

Susie opened the door behind him and came out on the porch. She was holding two thermoses in her hands. When Beau looked to her, she gave them to him and he nodded. Susie looked out at the storm.

"You're not going to find him out there in all this."

"I got to try."

"What if you can't?"

"It doesn't really feel like I'm going to miss him. Does it?"

She shook her head and wrapped her arms around herself from the cold.

He turned and looked to her standing there. "I'm coming back, hear?"

She shook her head again and looked downward. Beau stood holding the thermoses in his hands a few feet from her. He did not move towards her though the moment seemed to call for it. He felt then that it would have been something of an admission that he wanted no part of. That maybe there was no destiny set before him that was so subject to the power of the man and his words. He did not know in that instant if this was foolishness or worse, but that he had to believe it, and to believe that this was not going to be the last time that he saw her face in this world.

"I'll be back before the morning."

She moved towards him, but he turned from her and left down the steps, seeing out the corner of his eye that this stopped her. He walked down those stairs quickly until his boots met with the layer of snow that had accumulated atop the ground. A couple inches already. He stamped the snow beneath as he maintained this quick walk to the truck. He set the thermoses atop the cab as he opened up the truck. After putting the thermoses into the cup holders up front, he did stop and looked back at her on the porch. She was crying there, standing on the porch's edge, with light shining back from behind her, creating something of a halo around her figure. He looked for a moment with his throat tightening. He fought back any effect upon his face, though he knew that she could not have been able to see such a thing. He got in the truck and shut the door.

She watched the truck back out of the driveway until the dark enveloped its form, leaving only its headlights discernable, with sheets of snow falling before it. She watched as the truck backed out onto the road, skidding to a stop. It then lurched forward and drove off down the road. She watched it go. The light thrown out in front of the truck faded and then disappeared. She listened until she could hear it no more. She then waited some moments more in the quiet before turning back to the door and walking back into the house.

She closed the door behind her and reached for the lock out of habit, but as she grabbed it, she stopped and did not turn the lock shut. She was still sobbing some as she walked the hall to the kitchen and went in and turned on the light. Her heart felt in a sudden as if it had frozen within her chest as her eyes met with a figure sitting at the kitchen table. She shouted out and almost fell to the floor, leaning immediately to the counter to brace herself. The man did not react to this, sitting still and looking at her. His long black hair hung over the shoulders of his jacket, his eyes taking her in.

She stood there looking on at him as the rush of blood throughout her peaked and held steady with her heart throbbing audible to her. She put both hands on the edge of the counter to support her. Over these seconds she continued to look at him and him at her. He did not move. She gradually felt such rush subsiding and after several seconds could no longer hear her pulse. The man continued to sit still. His hands rested on the table in front of him. That's him, she thought, hearing her own voice within her mind.

"Do you want to sit down?" he asked in a calm tone.

She shook her head. Her nerves were only just coming back together.

"You going to run?"

She shook her head again.

"That's good," he said looking around the kitchen. "That's good."

"He did what you told him to," she said finally. "He's on his way out there to find you."

"He's on his way. But he's not doing what he has to do," the man said finishing his survey of the room, the pictures on the walls, the items hanging about. "Is he?"

She thought on how to respond to the man. "No. He's not," she said.

The man nodded, his hands still laying palm down on the table. "I'm curious as to what you make of him in all this. Have you come to a conclusion in your own mind?"

"Mister," she said, "I came to my conclusions about that man when I married him."

The man thought about that. "Has he told you about all this?"

"Yessir he has."

"About me?"

"Uh-huh."

The man nodded again. "And you think him innocent in this, do you?"

She stared at the man's eyes. And without having made any decision to do so, or at least that she felt, she leaned off of the counter and began walking to the other side of the kitchen table. She kept looking at the man as she did so. She pulled out the chair and sat down across from him and scooted herself in. She was surprised with what she had done, but felt herself calming. She did not know what to do with her hands, but settled them on the table.

"No sir."

"No sir what?"

"He isn't innocent. Not in any of it."

He measured this.

"I know him," she began again. "His soul. As far as men go – as far as people go – he's good, at his heart he is. But. But, within it all, he's broken. Broke like the rest of us."

"Broke?" the man asked.

"I don't know what word you'd prefer. Broke is how I always thought of it."

"Are you broke like him?"

"Yessir."

He continued to measure her. More and more curious.

"Are you stuck on the word? Is that it?"

"No."

"We all of us are broke. Bent. Bent is another word. That's a good word I think. Bent to go in a direction we aren't supposed to go. Towards things, and towards thoughts, I guess, we weren't intended to be part in."

The man's fingers tapped the table a few times. She looked to them.

"I don't know all that he's done mister. Or that you've done. I see he's bent up in all this and he's got stains all upon him and that he's scared."

"He's not the right kind of scared."

"No," she said.

"He wouldn't be driving out to the desert thinking that the demands upon him for such things can be overcome by anything but his blood," he said for the first time in a tone which came with some lack of restraint, with a wild beginning to come to his eyes.

"He's doing what desperate men do," she said.

The man let a quiet moment sit.

"But I don't think that's where his heart will stay," she said again.

"And you," the man asked, leaning ever so slightly forward, which she noticed with some greater fear coming upon her, "what is to become of you?"

She swallowed. "I'm not afraid of you, if that's what

you're asking."

This caused him to tilt his head a bit.

"Death has no sting left for me."

The man smiled at this. The smile stayed upon his face for several wretched seconds. The man then pushed himself backwards in his chair and then stood up. He looked down at her for a moment. The smile faded. He gave her a nod and then began walking out of the kitchen.

Susie sat still at the table as she listened to the steps of his boots leave the kitchen and go down the hall. She heard the door open and then heard it close. And then it was quiet again. She stayed seated. The ticking of the grandfather clock could be heard once again.

CHAPTER 18 – OUT IN THE DESERT

There was a half foot of snow on the ground out farther away from the house. Beau drove slow. There was nobody else on the roads. The snow continued to fall heavy, but without any wind to the storm. Like an immense sum of powder being poured out gently over the world around him. He could see but only a hundred feet in front of him within the beam of the headlights.

Beau kept slow as he made it to town. The town seemed like a thing deserted. A thing from the past. Stores were dark. Nobody was out. The cars that were still parked on Main Street had several inches of snow upon them. Beau knew the town would look much the same even if the storm had not come, as the people had heard something of what had come upon them.

Beau arrived at Coleman's house and parked and flashed the brights through the front window. It was a couple minutes before Coleman came out. He was also dressed in winter gear for hunting. Coleman's rifle was slung over his shoulder and he carried a shotgun in his hands. He walked across the yard and to the truck. Coleman opened the rear cab door and set down his rifle and shotgun parallel to Beau's rifle on the seat and shut the door. Coleman opened the front passenger door and looked at Beau from the outside for a moment. He then brushed the snow that had accumulated upon him off of himself and stepped up into the truck and closed the door behind him.

Coleman looked out the windshield at the snow-covered scene, at the masses of snow that continued to fall. "You still up for this?"

"What's out there isn't going to wait on all this. Sure as hell not us," Beau replied.

Beau looked to Coleman. Quiet for a moment. "I'm responsible for it. All of it. All we've seen today."

"What is it you're taking me to see?" Beau looked back out through the windshield. "I don't know how to describe him to you. All I really know about him is what he leaves behind. Though I've seen him."

Coleman's expression did not change. He stayed quiet, looking at Beau. Thinking. If there was any emotion present it was concern.

"You don't have to come. But if you do, you'll see him too. I don't know what that'll mean for me and you, but we'll have our chance."

"How do you know he'll be out there?"

"He told me so."

The snowfall was steady as they drove out of town and onto the highway that would lead them out to the canyons. The last time Beau had been on this highway, he had watched his father die. There were several inches of snow on the highway too. No one had driven upon it all night. They drove slow. There were no other cars.

When they were just about to the point on the highway where Senior had died, Beau saw something out ahead on the side of the road. As they came close to it, Beau pulled the truck off the highway and onto the shoulder. There were five crosses staked in the ground just off the highway of different sizes and kinds as a roadside memorial. There were dead arrangements and bouquets of flowers, mostly covered by the snow, laid out across the earth by the crosses.

The both of them stared at this lonely monument as the snow continued to fall all atop the crosses and heaps of flowers. They were quiet together for a moment. Coleman looked to Beau as if Beau might say something. Beau was quiet for a moment longer. He put the truck into drive and pulled back out onto the highway and drove on.

The storm kept on all through their drive out, which took them an hour. Coleman stayed quiet the whole time. His face disconcerted. But not like he was afraid of where they were going, but more that when he would look to Beau during this time, that he was afraid of Beau himself, or rather, what Beau had become, which was unknown.

Beau turned off onto the service road at mile marker 115 and began to drive the service road out to the desert. They drove another two miles on the service road until its end. Once they reached this end, Beau drove the truck to the road's edge and pointed the nose of the truck out toward the open desert and parked.

Beau thought on it. "We're going to have to walk from here."

The two of them got out of the truck and surveyed the world around them. The snowfall had lessened to a dusting of small flakes. There was a half-foot of snow on the ground, maybe more. The beams from the headlights showed the desert covered with white as far as the eye could see out into the night.

They opened up the back doors of the truck and took out their guns and readied them. Beau and Coleman secured the rifles upon their backs tight with slings. Coleman also grabbed his shotgun. Beau took off his cowboy hat and threw it in the back and pulled the beanie tight over his head. They both secured headlamps on their foreheads and turned them on, testing the beams that projected out into the night. Beau turned off the headlights of the truck and they both closed the doors. The desert which opened up before them bore a much darker pitch without the lights from the truck, pressing down heavy upon the two skinny beams from their heads.

They walked several feet in front of the truck and looked out. The tall outline of the first mesa head was about three miles out. Coleman and Beau looked at one another, Coleman's uncertainty was visible.

"I'm the only one that has to be here," Beau said.

Coleman looked out to the desert again. He marched forward. Beau followed.

They advanced through the snow side by side. The world around them was entirely quiet and still. Nothing in all creation moved. There were no tracks before them, but only some invisible path upon which they were being gently pulled by the gravity of the thing which awaited them. About a half-hour into the hike, the snowfall altogether stopped. The clouds above gradually broke over some minutes in a number of places, which allowed the moonlight through to the world. The white surface of the plains became bright with the moon's reflection. They turned off their headlamps.

"We even going the right way?" Coleman asked.

Beau looked around again. There was nothing printed on the snow for miles around them. "I don't think it matters."

They returned to walking. After about another half hour something caught Coleman's attention up ahead.

Beau then saw it too, out on the ground a couple hundred yards out. Beau took the binoculars from out of the pouch of his jacket and confirmed it. They adjusted their path forward towards that spot.

When they arrived, they saw that the markings on the snow were clear tracks of a single set of boots. The tracks headed off west across the plains. Looking out, it could be seen that within about two miles was the beginnings of the canyons. Beau unslung the rifle from off of his shoulder and removed rounds one-by-one from the pouch of his jacket and loaded them. Coleman did not do the same with his rifle, but stayed true to the shotgun already within his hands. Beau walked forward on the tracks.

Within thirty minutes, they were about a half mile out from the canyons. Beau stopped Coleman by the arm. He took out the binoculars again and looked out down the trail of prints, and there at what seemed to be the canyon's edge was a figure standing. He brought the binoculars into as much focus as he could and confirmed within himself that it was him. The figure was looking out over the canyon with its back to them. Beau could make out long black hair hanging down the figure's shoulders.

Beau handed the binoculars to Coleman and pointed to the spot. Coleman looked himself. When Coleman removed the binoculars, his face tightened with whatever was rising within him.

"That's him," Beau said.

They walked again with their guns in their hands and their eyes upon the figure out in the short distance at the canyon's edge, continuing to follow the thing's own footsteps. The figure remained still, looking out over the canyon in the opposite direction. As quiet as this world was, their steps, though deliberate and slow, were loud and obvious.

When they came within one-hundred yards, Beau stopped them. Beau knelt down on one knee and raised his rifle and pointed it at the figure. He looked down the barrel through the scope and saw the man clear. Same rawhide jacket and jeans as from the morning on the porch. He held the scope on the man for several seconds. The man did not move, but just kept on looking out over the canyon with his back towards them.

Beau lowered the rifle. He handed his binoculars once again to Coleman, who brought them to his eyes to look out at the man. "What we going to do?"

"Coleman. I'm going to shoot this thing."

Coleman lowered the binoculars, but still looked at the man. "That's a man."

Beau just looked at him.

"You're going to shoot the man in the back like that?" Coleman asked, his voice strained.

"I told you what he was."

Coleman was quiet.

"If he turns and sees us here. I'm telling you, he's going to kill us. Something awful," Beau said.

"I brought cuffs."

"Are you not hearing me?"

"He's a man."

Beau looked back to the figure and shook his head.

"The two of us. We got the drop on him dead to rights," Coleman said, "I mean, if he pulls on us, or puts up some fight, we do what we have to. But... You can't just shoot the man in the back. That ain't nothing but murder."

Beau was quiet for a moment. He then brought the rifle back up and took aim. The man was still facing away from them. Beau stared the man down with the sights square at the top-center of his back.

"Beau," Coleman said.

Beau continued his aim. Beau pushed the safety out, making a soft click.

"Beau," Coleman said in a raised voice now.

Another quiet moment passed with Beau locked on the man, confirming all things within himself. Coleman dropped the binoculars to the snow and leveled his shotgun at Beau's head four feet away. "Drop it!"

Beau did not move. His sight was undeterred. Coleman cocked the shotgun. Through the scope Beau did see the man now slowly turn about to face him. Not in a reactionary manner. But intentional. With a glare cold as death staring back through the scope.

Beau's rifle burst. The sights through the scope jolted and reset, and for a half second the man's glare remained upon Beau before the man's chest and head jerked backwards with the impact of the round. His body disappeared back over the edge of the canyon. Beau brought the rifle down and looked at the now empty spot beside the canyon.

Coleman took off running past Beau toward the canyon. After running about twenty yards, Coleman dropped his shotgun in the snow and kept on running with both arms free. Beau watched him run from his knelt position. Beau then got up and slung the rifle again back over his shoulder and secured it. Beau stepped over to where Coleman had been standing and leaned down and picked up the binoculars. He walked out after Coleman towards the canyon from where the man had fallen.

Coleman fell to all fours at the edge and looked down to the canyon floor. Beau's walk brought him to a few feet behind Coleman after a very long minute. Beau stood behind him for a moment. He then walked to the edge beside Coleman and looked over.

The floor was some four-hundred feet or so down. The moonlight hit the floor clear. Sprawled out there directly below them was the figure. Beau put the binoculars to his eyes. The man had hit the floor directly on his back. His arms and legs were stretched out in random angles and were crooked. The man's dark hair was spread out about his head like a grim halo. Nothing about him moved. He was dead.

Beau removed the binoculars and looked over at Coleman. Coleman was no longer looking down at where the man lay, but was now looking out over the canyon stretched beyond.

"We murdered that man."

"You haven't seen what I've seen."

"Haven't I?"

"No. You have not."

"So tell me what he was then. You look at him there."

Beau did not respond.

"My God," Coleman said more softly, shaking his head.

Coleman took the beanie off of his head and pulled off his gloves. He pressed both his hands flat over his face and held them there. He then ran his fingers like clawed combs through his hair to the back of his scalp. Coleman then clawed those fingers back forward through his hair the other direction. He returned to all fours and pushed his hands, with fingers spread wide, down into the snow by his knees.

Beau stood measuring what was becoming of Coleman. "It was him."

Coleman shook his head more. "You used me."

"I what?"

"So that you wouldn't have to do whatever this was alone. From whatever in the hell you're into."

"Slow this down."

"Responsible, you said, right? You were responsible for what happened to them. Explain that again to me. Or did you even try the first time, I can't remember?"

Beau stepped back two steps from him and the canyon's edge. Whatever was unraveling, continued to do so in the quiet between them as Coleman stared down into the snow.

"'Cause I put him back into the world," Beau said.

Coleman looked up to him now. "Can you hear yourself?"

"I showed him to you. That's what I told you I would do."

Coleman just stared up at him. Coleman looked back out over the canyons and shook his head more. It was quiet again.

The vision of the man took hold of Beau. Beau stepped back to the edge of the canyon and dropped to his knees and steadied himself again. He looked down through the binoculars at the man again.

"Look at him again," Beau said to Coleman, extending

the binoculars.

"Put that shit away," Coleman said with a raised hand held as if in a stopping motion.

Beau held the binoculars out still. "Look."

Coleman sighed. He reached out and took the binoculars and steadied himself at the edge and looked down.

Beau took the rifle from off of his back and placed it on the snow. He unlatched the scope from the top of the rifle and took it within his hand and leaned back over to the edge. Beau looked down at the man lying there through the scope.

"See that?" Beau asked.

Coleman kept looking down. "See what?"

"Blood?"

Coleman kept looking. He raised up a bit. The broken body of the man was without any sign of blood upon it. Neither did the snow around him show anything of the substance.

And the man's arm moved. And then it jerked again. Coleman shouted out at the second movement. And with a shake, each of the man's limbs began to writhe and contort, as if made of many different pieces pulling back together, slithering as it were upon the ground. Then his head wrenched back and forth. Then back and forth again more violently. Then the whole of the man rose upwards to standing, with everything snapping back to with a crack, that though muffled, was audible to them above. Coleman shouted out again.

Standing settled, the man looked up at the both of them. The edge of the man's glare upon them could be felt. The man walked slowly forward to the base of the wall of the canyon some ten feet away. He put his hands upon it, groping about as if for a grip. He then pulled himself upwards and with this momentum began crawling quickly up the wall like some horrible spider. The man's face was set upon them with his belly pressed flat upon the wall, and with his arms and legs bent outwards unnatural as the limbs fired back and forth in stride. His head did not move, even with such frantic pace. He would be at the top within the minute.

Beau dropped the scope from his eye and looked up to his friend. Coleman was frozen in place, looking down through the binoculars at the creature ascending towards them. "Coleman," Beau said, and then again more loudly, "Coleman!" Beau grabbed Coleman by the arm and pulled him back away from the canyon's edge with Coleman backpedaling until he finally looked to Beau and caught his balance and turned and began to run.

Coleman got out in front. Coleman ran straight past his shotgun in the snow. Beau leaned down as he ran past and grabbed the gun by the barrel and kept on. The two ran like children, with the sight of the thing's crawl up the canyon filling them with that terror that causes one to let go of thought altogether, with that pain in their chests coursing down through all nerves to their limbs, which flailed without any restraint. They ran back across their own tracks, which were now interwoven with the man's from before, and they saw with each step the path that had led them to what would be their deaths. The half foot of snow upon the earth was unstable and different with each step, adding a heaviness to each such step that was subtle, but accumulating.

The desert stretched out before them was empty with no landmark to run towards. Sterile and hopeless was the sight of the distance, and if they had not just traveled such route, it would have seemed a path to nothing but more of the beyond, which could not be covered before they had been devoured.

The futility of their current course hit Beau all in a moment. Coleman himself looked like some fool running frantically before him. Without consciously making the decision, Beau found himself stopped and watching Coleman run away from him down the tracks. As Beau watched him go, he saw how slow such progress really was. Beau continued to watch Coleman as he felt the pace of his breathing begin to slow, and with it, a pain swept across his chest like a wave. Beau dropped the shotgun in the snow and put his hands to his knees, recovering in each moment with such pain heavy within him. As his thought returned, he noticed that the rifle was no longer on his back, but had been dropped some distance ago. And for yet another time in the past days, he realized he was going to die.

Beau turned back the other direction to where the man would come for him. There he was only a few hundred yards off, running across the snow fluid and powerful. Though Beau could not see his face, he was terrified by the thought of it, as whatever dark power that had been restrained behind it was now free. But unlike moments similar to this one in recent days, Beau was not afraid for himself. His feelings were for Coleman. Who he knew to be running still across the desert behind him, likely realizing by now that hope was not a thing which existed in that place. Beau looked back behind him on the ground and found the shotgun. He walked quickly to it and picked it up.

Beau looked again back to the man. He was only a hundred yards off now and would be there in moments. Beau cocked the shotgun. He stepped back his right foot and brought the butt of the gun to his shoulder and leveled it at the charging creature.

The man ran and ran in a rush, with his steps upon the ground making thuds which could now be heard. Beau found himself holding his breath and devoting all his strength to the steadying of his hands and to fighting off the growing urge to flinch at the momentum of the force that was about to meet with him, which was expanding in the air and taking hold of him. The man's eyes were now visible and put a weight behind the urge to flinch. At the final moment before the man's outstretched hands would meet with him – he fired.

The man became a flash which jutted to the side and then hit Beau like a truck, with the man's grasp taking hold of Beau within such collision like some vise. Beau did not fly off after the impact. Beau found as he opened his eyes that he was travelling across the snow at great speed upon his back. Beau's shoulder ached deep with a sharp pain, and as he looked to it, he saw the man's hand grasped tight around his clavicle with the man's fingertips pushing deep down into the coat.

The man's grip was like a pin through Beau's body that caused a pain that prevented the rest of his body from moving. All he could move was his left arm on the other side, but just barely, and with no strength that could affect what was happening to him. Beau could see from the ground behind them speeding by that they were still traveling upon the path of the tracks.

All Beau could do was look up at the sky whirling by. The friction of his body over the sheet of snow and ice kicked up a mist of frost that stung his face, making a sound like a strong wind. Though Beau tried as he could, he could not angle his head to see anything. The man's grip into the meat and bone of his shoulder forced him prostrate and helpless. Beau could still only move his other arm. Beau put his hand upon the man's hand gripping his shoulder as it was all he could do. But the man's hand was like steel. And so Beau flailed helplessly, trying to breathe as best he could.

Beau heard a scream somewhere within the mixture of noise around him. In that moment before the impact, he pictured Coleman's face. And for but a flash how he imagined Coleman's father had appeared in that dream looking on at him. The man's hand stayed clamped upon Beau's shoulder as the man collided with Coleman. The jolt from this brake in speed made Beau's stomach drop as the lower half of his body folded upward into his chest before falling again to the earth.

Beau felt then the release of the pressure around his shoulder, though it left a throbbing pain still. But before Beau could think to move, a heaviness pressed down upon the center of his chest and compressed it nearly flat, now pinning him to the snow, as if the edge of some great weight had tipped onto him, driving all that mass through this center point. The man was standing upon his chest with one boot. The man held Coleman up into the air above himself with one hand gripping Coleman's throat with outstretched arm. The man's face was wild, like a beast about to swallow him whole. Coleman struggled as he could with the man's hand in futility, his legs squirmed in the air like a beetle's might when upon its back, kicking about for some footing that would not be found.

The man looked down to Beau. The moon set the man's eyes alight. With a voice distinct from what Beau had heard before, deep and other-worldly, the man said "you did this." A loud crack sounded within the man's hand around Coleman's throat. Warm liquid sprayed across Beau's face, causing him to shut his eyes. Beau tasted the iron-laden tang of the blood. He could not allow himself to look up to what must have been left of Coleman.

The weight of Coleman's body fell upon the snow beside Beau.

The man leaned down with his foot still driven into Beau's chest, compressing it all the more. He brought his face down within inches of Beau's face. Beau turned his face away. The man said in a soft voice, "look at me."

After a moment, Beau did. The man's eyes were Beau's view entire. And in this same voice, the man said, "There's only one way."

The weight left Beau's chest. He fell over to his side, coughing and sucking in the frigid air. The man grabbed Beau by his shoulder and side, picked him up into the air several feet, and then threw him out over the snow back towards the canyons. Beau hit the ground heavy on the top of his back and skidded across the snow, spinning until his movement stopped.

For many minutes Beau could do nothing but lie there, coughing, getting back his breath. His chest and shoulder ached deep into the muscle and tissue and bone. The feeling returned to his face with a sting, and with this feeling he could sense again the substance upon it. He wiped his cheek with his hand and opened it before his eyes to see the black residue of Coleman's blood smeared over his open palm and fingers. Beau laid back his head and looked up at the sky. He could still feel the man's presence a short distance away. He stared upwards some more moments.

"Get to it," the man said some ways away out of view.

Beau rolled over onto his side again, grimacing from the pain. Then he rolled some more to his chest. He pushed himself to his hands and knees. Through the pain he pushed himself up from there to standing. He wobbled as he found his balance upon his feet. The man waited twenty feet back up the path of tracks towards the direction of the truck. The man stared at him quietly.

Beau turned back toward the canyons. He saw the path led back a half mile to the edge. He thought again of the man's demand of him and saw the end of his life there. Beau began to walk this path again.

Beau looked downwards upon the tracks of the path as he went. He could see the desperate steps that they had left while running from the man, intermixed with the calm track of their walk toward the man from before, when Beau thought they would kill him. Men walking towards a lie, and then running from the truth. Beau looked back every so often and saw the man walking out behind him still at a distance of twenty feet.

When Beau reached the canyon, he walked directly to its edge. He looked out over its wide mouth and the drop below. He stared it down for some moments. Thinking. As he saw the space between him and the ground below to which he would fall, the torment of those seconds, his death, he knew the man was right. That his demand was true. And that he deserved the fall.

He stood for a moment longer. But he turned back toward the man. The man studied him with the same blank expression. Beau looked to him, and then to the ground. When Beau looked up again, the man was gone. Back towards the world. Back to her.

Beau began to jog fast as he could after him down the path.

CHAPTER 19 – INFERNO

- Beau

Dad prayed with me each night beside my bed before I would go to sleep. He prayed always for the Lord. For His glory. And for us to be some small part in such a tremendous thing, and that this would make our souls content and happy. He prayed for His name. He prayed for things to happen in the future that God had promised from thousands of years ago. I did not know that other people prayed mostly for themselves until I was much older and found that a peculiar thing for a great while.

Towards the end of such prayers he would ask permission to speak to Sam. He would tell Sam that he missed him with all his heart, though he was happy for him to be with Jesus. That his thoughts were always of him, in some way or another. That he was so proud to have been his daddy, proud to still be his daddy. He said that someday after we were all in heaven together for a thousand years that the sting of this time apart would no longer be remembered. Dad was not afraid to cry in front of me, and did so often during these times.

The man walked down the middle of Main Street in the heart of the small town. It was altogether dark, with light coming only from the dim street lamps that lined the road. The man looked over the various shops of all kinds, the diner, the bank, the laundromat, all closed and dark.

Everything was covered in several inches of snow. There were only a few cars parked on the sides of the street.

The man stopped in the road and turned around, looking at it all. One particular shop caught his attention. He walked across the road to the sidewalk and up to the front display window of the shop. On the glass it read in a golden font, "Bettie's Antiques And Treasures." Through the window the man saw groupings of old furniture, clocks, paintings, old books, different trinkets, dolls, and toys of all kinds. Bits and pieces of people's lives, each with some different part captured and embodied in the thing, up for interpretation.

The man noticed the distorted outline of his reflection upon the glass, visible only in part by the streetlamp from behind him on the sidewalk. The man stared down the man looking back at him. The man took his left hand and laid it palm down against the wall to the side of the store's front window. He pressed against the wall, looking at his hand.

A flame ignited beneath and then over his hand. This blue and yellow flame then spread out from his hand across the wall as ink might when poured upon a page. The flames traveled quickly up and down the wall, and in a moment, the entire front of the store was ablaze.

The man walked down the sidewalk to the next store. After he passed the display window of that store to its front wall, he reached out with two extended fingers and drug them across the wall as he walked. A streak of flame was left upon the wall. The flame began to run up and down the wall as it had before.

The man walked in this same manner to the next store and drug his entire hand across that wall, smearing flame across it as well, and as before, the flame spread quickly outward until it covered the entire front of the store, running to the roof above and out of view.

The man did the same to the next shop, and then the next, and then the next, until he had reached the end of that side of Main Street. He turned and looked back at this side of the road. All the buildings were engulfed in the blue and yellow flame and were quickly being digested within it. The flames shot high into the night, dancing, jumping to other buildings nearby, beginning the consumption of them as well.

The man looked to the other side of the road at all the shops waiting there. They were aglow with an orange hue from the walls of fire towering over them from across the street, looking small, and cowering.

The man crossed Main Street in his casual stride to the first of these shops. He reached out with the pointer finger of his right hand and jabbed its front wall, leaving a spot of yellow, which ran out in all directions from this center. He walked again by each of the buildings and shops on this side of the street and touched their front walls or doors with this finger, igniting each of them in the same fashion, sparing none, until he had also reached the end of this side of the road.

When it was done, he turned and looked over the scene. The center of the town burned within his fire. The air around him was cooking with the intensity of the heat, which only grew with each moment. He walked to the edge of the sidewalk here and sat down on the curb and waited. He smiled to himself.

People began to show up within ten minutes. The first were individuals, coming on foot. Then small groups came. And then cars began to arrive and park wherever they could out past the edge of Main Street. The people congregated all at the edge of the street. Their faces were bright and florid from the fire consuming their lives before them. Women cried. Shouts sprang out among them. They did not move much at all. They only huddled and beheld the spectacle, their numbers multiplying by the minute, adding nothing but more mass to the sorry crowd. Some of them could be seen pointing to the man sitting on the curb at the center of the inferno. He looked on at them.

Beau could see the fire from fifteen miles out on the highway. His heart sank within him. "Please," he said aloud in the empty cab. "Please."

When Beau drove the top of the incline on the hill just before town, he pulled over to the side of the road and got out of the truck. The entire downtown was ablaze like a candle, spouting flames high above which swirled about. Beau brought both palms to the sides of his temples. The thought came to his mind that the man could be leaving countless dead within his fire. Beau got back into the truck and sped off on the highway, with the back wheels and bed fishtailing a bit over the snow-packed road. Beau turned on the red and blues atop the truck.

The man remained seated and still on the sidewalk in the middle of the wildfire. More and more people pointed at him. Whatever sounds the crowd was making could not be heard above the noise coming from the fire and its boiling contents, a noise which had grown as extreme as the heat.

Red flashing lights appeared behind and slightly above the crowd. The crowd parted and let the fire engine roll slowly through. The engine stopped at the edge of the street as those that steered it got out and took in the sight of the fire before them and conferred. The fire engine remained parked for some minutes. The man watched it.

The fire engine rolled forward past the outer edge of Main Street and travelled down the road between the two walls of flame churning on both sides. The fire engine traveled this path delicately, its windows reflecting the world around it a fierce orange. The truck came to about twenty feet in front of the man and stopped. The flashing red lights atop the fire engine were something pathetic within this world and the powers of the colors that danced all around them.

The man stood up. He walked to the center of the street and stopped. He stared at the truck and its inhabitants with a glare that of a warning. The doors of the fire engine opened and eight men came out in their bright yellow gear, with masks and helmets atop their heads hiding their faces. They moved slow and took position in a huddle at the side of the truck, all with their faces set upon the man. A few of them had axes in their hands. They stood there looking at the man, as if this were their opening statement, and awaiting a reply.

The man began to walk the short distance between them. His face showed no effect from the heat. He was calm. As the man reached and then walked past that point ten feet in front of the huddle of men, they each took steps backward in an increasingly desperate attempt to match the man's approach. A couple of them bumped into each other within this backpedal as they scrambled back with each of the man's steps.

The man reached the driver's side door of the fire engine and stopped his march forward. The huddle of men stopped their retreat a few moments later, now some twenty feet back behind the truck. The man stared them down. A moment passed between them as the man's eyes seemed to drink them in, alive with the potential for violence with each of them.

The man looked to his side at the fire engine. He stepped to it and put both hands upon it palm down with crooked fingers as if his fingertips dug down into the truck's metallic skin. The men stared on. Flames burst forth from the places where the man's fingers gripped the truck and spread down its sides in all directions, rolling like a wave upon its surface. The men scrambled backwards again several feet. In seconds, the entirety of the fire engine was wrapped in fire, with its cherry red exterior quickly bubbling like a stew. The flames sucked up this cherry red color and swirled and spun about.

The man remained attached to the truck by his hands pressed to its side. The man's rawhide jacket caught fire and dissolved in seconds, with such flames disappearing. The man's jeans caught fire as well, and parts of them too began to dissolve within such flames. The man took his hands off of the truck and turned toward the men and walked forward again for several steps. The fire on his clothes disappeared as vapors rose off of the man. The remnants of his clothes still clung to his body in several places, while at other places his bronze skin showed, glistening, but not burned. His black hair waved as he walked, intact and unharmed. The man's face kept its wild glare, gleaming with something like sweat, but without burn.

The man stopped his walk again, staring at these men still retreating from him and whatever ideas they had brought with them down this road when they first approached. The fire engine exploded behind the man, spewing flames upwards and out in all directions. The man was unmoved, looking out at the men. Each of the men flew back some feet from the force and noise and surprise of it and fell to the asphalt hard. Whatever had been in their hands flew free in various directions and went skidding and spinning across the street. Some of their helmets, with masks attached, ejected from atop their heads and rolled across the street as well. None of them stayed on the ground for more than an instant, as each of them sprung upwards and stumbling as they turned and ran back toward the crowd, which was screaming at the sight of it all. Not a man looked back.

The man watched them run before him all the way until they met the crowd, with several people stepping forward to receive them. The man looked down at his body at what remained of his clothes. His jeans were largely intact, though charred black. He peeled off the shreds of shirt and jacket that stuck to his skin until his torso was bare. The man bent over and took off each of his boots and tossed them to the side of him. The man then sat down in the middle of the street, with hands coming to rest upon his knees, and he drew still, staring at the crowd down the road with a calm coming over his face. The flames towered and roared at each side of the street beside him. Random structures in the fire collapsed at various spots along the street, though such collapses only made the fire rise all the more with a heightened brightness.

Beau saw the crowd out in the distance as he drove into town on the road that would become Main Street. The other squad cars and trucks were parked with lights flashing down the street before the beginnings of the crowd. The cars were deserted, with none of the deputies around. Beau drove by slow, the crowd still some fifty yards ahead.

As Beau reached the rear of the crowd, people turned, having noticed the flashing lights. Their faces showed fear like one only sees upon the television. The sight of it in reality was something strange. Beau's truck came to a stop just short of the crowd. Many of those who noticed him alerted others around them and the crowd began to separate and create a channel through on the road. Beau waited and watched this separation progress down the line. As the peoples separated, he put the truck in park and turned the engine off. The people nearby were all staring at him dumbfounded through the windshield, and he imagined those in the distance whose faces he could not see bore something the same.

Beau opened the door and got out and stood at the side of his truck, looking at those around him. He looked to the ground and thought a moment. Beau took the beanie from off of his head and pulled the camouflaged hunting jacket off over his head as well, which took with it the two other layers of sweaters he had underneath. He prevented the plain white t-shirt from coming off. Beau balled the jacket and sweaters and threw them in the back seat and straightened up the t-shirt upon his torso as best he could. He got his cowboy styled sheriff's hat from the backseat and put it upon his head. He saw his sidearm holster on the floor of the backseat and stared at it for a moment. He left it there and shut the door.

When he looked back to the faces of the crowd, all of them were looking to him, quiet, varying some with shock, others with something of pity, but all terrified of what was enveloping all around them, though they remained. Beau walked down the channel that the crowd had made. Coleman's dried blood still stained Beau's face. When he started this walk, he looked around to receive these glares, but as he continued, he could take them no longer and kept his eyes focused straight ahead as those still on the center of the road continued to catch the cue and moved to the side to allow his passage.

The crowd continued to divide all the way through until he had reached its front at the beginnings of Main Street. Beau saw several of his deputies at the front in plain clothes, holding the line of the crowd at the street. Their faces bore the same fear as the others. He kept walking through and looked down the street and saw the man sitting there. The man rose and stood on the spot.

The heat even from where Beau stood was intense. He wondered if it was possible to go any further, though he knew he had no choice. He walked towards the man. The walls of fire on both sides brought forth an overwhelming sound of the fire rushing, and whirling, and whipping about. The buildings burning and dismantling.

The man looked like a native warrior from ages past. Raw and ancient, gorgeous and lethal. His face and bare chest glistened and glowed crimson from the fire over and around them. His black hair was free. His eyes were wild and set upon Beau and his future. Beau slowed his pace careful and deliberate at about fifteen feet from the man, walking reluctant with each step to see if the man would allow further progress until Beau stopped altogether five feet short.

"Do you understand yet?" the man asked.

Beau looked around at the heart of his town being consumed by the man's fire. In the brightness Beau's eyes could be seen moist and reflecting the power of the light. Coleman's dried blood almost shining red.

"The things you do become part of this world." The man looked around at the raging fire. "Maybe it's more like the things which you are become part of this world. They must be spoken for. It's all I've wanted for you."

"You think it deserved all this do you?"

"It's what all of you deserve. I just showed it to you."

"You should've killed me down in that cellar. Should've killed me right then."

"You don't understand at all then, do you?"

"I don't."

"What has to be paid, can't be taken."

Beau shook his head.

"Don't you see what I've done for you?"

"Done for me? What you've done for me?"

"I've shown you the truth that all the world has hidden. All these people. Since there has been man and since there has been time."

"All I've seen is evil. And death." Beau looked again at all that fire, which only grew in the momentum of its noise and strength.

"But that is the truth, isn't it? That your choices are evil. That they bring evil to the world from thin air. Taken from the dark down in you, given teeth, and set loose to the world. For a multitude of reasons that are but one reason."

Beau stared at the man.

"That you all love what is in the dark more than you think you could love the truth. And you lie to yourselves about what it is. About whether there is a judge that could tell you what it is. Until there is no judge, and there is no truth, and there is no price. The price. That's what I am."

The man stared at Beau. There was a crash out in the flame from some structure giving way. Beau closed his eyes.

"You knew what you had coming. But you ran. Down into the dark. Where you chose what you wanted the truth to be. And your choice was set free, and you dropped its chains, and pointed it up to the light, to the world. And then it became a part of it. And did what all monsters from the dark do."

Beau opened his eyes.

"And require what all such things require." The man stepped forward to Beau, face to face. He looked at him, measuring if Beau could doubt a word that he had said. "Which can't be taken. Only paid."

The man stepped to Beau's side and walked past him several feet. The man then stopped. He turned back to Beau. "Those who see the truth of what they are, see their need. Pity the blind." The man nodded toward the crowd

213

of people looking on. "Everyone's souls are a burning." The man turned and walked away on the road toward the crowd. Beau stood on the spot still and watched him go.

Screams came from the crowd as he walked toward them. Some started running in various directions away from the street. Many more stayed still in shock, though a similar channel through the crowd formed rapidly for the approaching figure. The man walked fearless and without guilt and without care as to what harm this pathetic mob could do. He walked right through their midst, each of them looking at the man as a coward would. Like a whole world of cowards afraid to look at the thing walking around in reality.

As the man was about to pass the very end of the crowd, an older cowboy reached out from where he stood and grabbed the man passing by at the elbow. The man stopped and looked to his elbow and then to the face of the older man. The older man's face was certain. But he let the man's elbow go and the older man's arm fell to his side. The man stared at the older man for a moment longer and then he walked out of the end of Main Street and kept straight on a smaller road that led out of town, out to the dark of the world.

None in the crowd moved. They all looked at each other. Someone at the front of the crowd hollered out. Everyone in the crowd looked back toward the burning town.

Beau was walking back to them and had almost reached the front of the crowd. His face had lost any color to it and his walk became unsteady. His eyes circled about, trying to focus on something out in front of him, and his hands went up in front of him as a blind person's might, feeling around for some obstacle in front of him. Beau stumbled forward and lost his balance entirely and collapsed upon the street. The crowd shouted out collectively and many rushed to attend to him.

- Beau

Since Grandad did most all of his preaching on the road, I did not actually get to see him on the pulpit that many times. Dad did this one time take me with him to a small gathering outside of Tucson where Grandad was to preach. There were only about twenty in the crowd, including Dad and me, and Grandad spoke to each of us, looking to our eyes as if in personal conversation.

He said one of his favorite comparisons that Christ used for Himself was the serpent pole out in the wilderness used to save God's people. The peoples had been wicked, and God had sent fiery serpents to bite them, so that many died. When the peoples began to repent, Moses cried out to God, and the Lord told him to make a fiery serpent and set it on a pole, and that all who had been bitten who looked to such figure would live. Moses did make such fiery serpent out of bronze and put it on a pole, and as the Lord had promised, all who looked to it lived. And as Jesus said, as Moses lifted up the serpent in the wilderness, so must He be lifted up, that whoever believes in Him may have eternal life.

Grandad himself was fiery that afternoon. The building, with no working air conditioning, must have matched the 105-degree heat outside. And Grandad kept yelling that we need only look to the resurrected Christ for healing and we would be healed. Look to Him! Look! Look! Look! We are all of us snakebit and poisoned, but if we would only look to Him, keep on looking at Him, we would be healed. And he looked dead at me on his final word – Look!

The doctor told Susie that Beau had collapsed on account of exhaustion and dehydration. A shock to the system he called it. Distress, he said. They had given him medications to keep him asleep and resting, though as he lay unconscious in the bed, his closed eyes periodically twitched, and his face would spasm now and again as if some struggle remained within his mind that would not let him go. The room was kept dark aside from a small lamp like something of a nightlight across the room from where Beau laid.

Three deputies that had been at the scene waited outside the room in the hallway of the medical center in plain clothes and told Susie about all that had happened in town. Two state troopers in uniform were also in the hallway when Susie arrived, though they did not speak with her. They had watched over him from the hallway, talking with each other. They left after a half-hour.

Susie told the doctor that she needed to be there in the room with him. The doctor said it was best to let him alone and rest, and that he would not be awake for many hours from what they were giving him, though she wouldn't have it, and he agreed to let her in alone so long as she tried nothing to wake him.

The sight of Beau there alone in that room and struggling beneath the artificial sleep overwhelmed her with the loneliest feeling she could remember in her life. A loneliness for him and where he now existed, though he was still the man she loved with all her soul, and though he seemed in some far off place within what thoughts had hold of him, he was still close to her.

She dragged a cushioned chair from against the wall over next to his bedside and sat watching over him. The nightlight cast a soft and dimmed yellow upon him. His torso was inclined in an angle upward in the hospital bed. His face continued to twitch and nod every so often and his mouth would open a bit as if at the beginning of whispering something, though it would only close again. He had an IV running out of his arm to a drip bag above and some other cords running to a machine and a screen that showed his vitals. He wore a white gown with a faded checkered print from unnumbered washes, worn by the many others she thought that had lived and died through such traumas. She cried quietly for several minutes looking on at him.

An older woman in scrubs opened the door at the side of the room and leaned in. "Shift change ma'am," she said in a quiet voice. "You need anything?"

Susie wiped the tears from her face and looked to her, "thank you. No, I don't think so. Not right now."

"You want something to drink honey? I got bottles of water down at the station there."

"No thank you."

"Okay then. Name's Loraine if you need anything, I'm down the hall. Somebody'll be by in about a half-hour to check in with more of the medications, okay?"

Susie nodded.

"Okay," she said and she closed the door softly.

Susie looked back at him. "My Lord," she said aloud in the quiet.

A chill came over her and she noticed for the first time how cold the room was. The skin on her forearms bore goosebumps all up and down. She got up from the chair and crawled into the bed beside him, being careful not to put any weight upon him. She wedged herself between him and the bedrail at his side and watched his face. There was no reaction from him. She shifted herself up against his side and laid her face on the pillow next to his. She brought her hand up and gently rested it on top of his arm, feeling his warm skin against her own.

She laid there and watched him, breathing a slow and gentle cadence. She felt his arm twitch beneath her cupped hand and held it steady until such twitches subsided. As she looked upon his face there, she saw within it the sum of all the years of their lives. And though this place they were in now was dark in so many ways, the sum tone from such calculation was warm and familiar to her, a thing not outweighed or taken by the place in time they now resided. She decided that it never would be and it was a comfort to her. The sum of him, and of them, would be good always to her, though stained on its surfaces, its truth beneath a thing she knew unassailable.

"You aren't lost to me," she said just above a whisper. "There is nowhere I could not find you." She laid her head upon his shoulder and continued to watch him.

The door opened a half-hour or so later, letting a harsh light cut through the tender tone of darkness in which she had grown comfortable within the room. Such light expanded on Beau's face like a searchlight. The world without would not let their place together there exist for but a short collection of moments. It does not allow anyone to survive. A young man in scrubs and a hoodie walked over to the other side of the bed and looked down at them with something of empathy upon his face. She looked up at him. He looked as if he might say something to her.

This man worked at a spot on Beau's other arm which had a tube inserted like that of his IV. He injected a syringe full of a pale pink liquid through this tube into his arm and then removed the syringe and capped the tube. The man went to the bottom of the bed by Beau's feet and picked up a clipboard from the cubby. The man looked to the screen above, then back and forth, and scribbled things down upon paper atop the clip board. He then put the clipboard back into the cubby and stood there looking down at them. The pity returned to his face as he measured them there. He began to walk back to the door of the room and lifted his hand up at her, holding it there until he reached the door. He turned and backed out of the room as he closed the door behind him delicately, taking with him the light from out of the hallway.

She was again left with Beau in the dark of the room, with the nightlight by the wall providing a soft accent of isolation. She returned her eyes to Beau's face and laid still watching him. She removed her hand from his arm and rested it upon his chest at that spot over his heart, watching his face carefully for any agitation, though there was none.

His chest raised slowly upward with breath beneath her palm, expanding and at last holding still at capacity, and then sank downward and rested flat, again holding still, before rising again, with pulsing heart within always thumping. She saw a clock in her mind, and it ticked in sync with this rhythm, counting down the time left. She resolved to quiet her mind there and let herself simply feel and observe each passing moment. Though there was no action or narrative to the scene in which she found herself, she drank it in deeply like a thing which could be savored. The fragility of the thing. A piece of time she would make part of herself.

She laid there with her eyes open, hand upon his heart, as the time ran. It ran slow, as it can when one decides that it is so. Three hours went by before the light of the room began to change from what was coming in through the window behind the curtains at the side of the room. This time was ending. The world was again awakening. She removed her hand carefully from his chest. She laid there feeling full and satisfied and grateful. She leaned her body off of his side and scooted up against the bedrail. She then slid herself down across the bed until her legs could be extended out over its side, and with a continuing slide she lowered her feet down to the floor and sat up on the side of the bed. She pushed down on her palms and raised herself to standing.

She saw on a countertop at the side of the room a clear pitcher filled with water, with paper Dixie cups stacked ten high to its side. She walked to the counter and poured herself a full cup and drank it down. She set the cup down and saw on the counter Beau's clothes folded in a small pile. She saw also Beau's keys, and watch, and wedding ring beside the clothes. She took the ring in her hand. She closed her hand around it and stood holding it. Feeling its meager weight, though weight there was.

She walked back to the bedside and looked down on him. His face was of a shifting character as the light of the world was advancing upon it. She reached down and took his hand within her hands, holding it in the air for a moment. She then held it up within one of her hands and used the other to slide the ring upon his finger. It slid without resistance down to the finger's base. She placed his hand back down upon the covers of the bed.

She backed away out of the room, looking at him, until she reached the door, where she turned and took hold of the handle. She opened it quietly and stepped out and turned to shut it behind herself. Through the opening of the doorway which closed before her she saw him vanishing there until the door was closed.

Beau slept in this state another hour until the light of the morning was full within the room and he awoke. He sat up in the bed groggy and without any thoughts coming together. He looked down upon himself and took inventory of the IV coming from his arm, along with the patches attached to other places upon his arms and the wires that ran out over the bed's edge and then upwards. He looked out over the room, foreign and confusing, as he sorted through the fog upon his mind. He stretched his hands out in front of his face and opened them. He looked to his open palms and fingers as if there would be some answer upon them. He saw his ring there upon his finger and stared at it. And in a sudden the weight of all that reality landed back upon his mind with the brunt of its body entire.

His eyes closed as such weight settled upon him with a dull pain that pressed down deep within, which did restrict his breath for those first few moments. He opened his eyes and again saw the ring upon his finger and stared at it. He sat still calculating it all.

Beau looked up again at the room around him with his mind now in tune with his present state. He knew it to be a room at the medical center. His mind brought back those last moments. The man. His words. The fire. The heat. The people. The dead. His wife. Susie. He felt a new pain in his heart. For her. It was a pain which moved him down the bed and to standing.

The tubes and wires running from off of his body snapped taut. He looked down upon these parts of his arm and removed the IV with no care to what it was and without care as to the pain that came from it. He also peeled off the patches with their wires and dropped such things to the floor swinging.

He looked again around the room until he found his piled clothes upon the counter at the side. He made for them while pulling the gown off of himself. He saw with relief his keys there beside the clothes. He put back on his underwear and pants, and then straightened up the shirt and pulled it over his head, smelling at once the bitter and sharp odor that his body had left through the night before, mixed with the smoke, bringing an acrid taste to his mouth as if he had suddenly been made to drink the existence of such consequences full and tangible. As the shirt came set upon him, he saw a vision of Coleman laid out on the snow, with a black substance across the ground, and with eyes open wide and dulled, himself broken and poured out and gone. And the pain for her returned again with a deeper bite within.

Why was she not here?

Beau picked up his keys from off of the table and pushed them down in his pants pocket. He picked up his hat with the other hand. He saw his watch there but did not grab it before turning to find the door at the other side of the room. He walked quickly to it. As he grabbed its handle, the thought came to him that he did not know what conclusions had been made through the night and that a great deal might depend upon him leaving this place without being noticed. With such thought settling, he turned the knob slowly and pulled the door open but a few slow inches.

He looked out at what he could see in the hallway, but nothing could be seen. He opened the door a full two feet and looked. There was no one directly outside the room. He stuck his head out and looked down the hall one way and then the other, there were two nurses down at the other end of the hall standing outside a room and talking to one another without any notice of him. He looked to the other end of the hall again and saw the double doors and the exit sign above. He looked back over to the nurses in their conversation, with them still not looking over. He stepped out into the hall and walked quickly for the doors in the other direction, putting his cowboy hat with the county sheriff's emblem at its center on top of his head. He walked to these doors without looking back, with some tension rising within him as he waited for someone to shout out at him, though no such shouts came. He made it to the doors and pushed one of them open and walked out of the unit.

Beau kept his head mostly down and staring at some point off on the floor as he walked the halls and through larger areas and then to the lobby. People walked around him, but nobody engaged him or stopped him. At last he saw in the top corners of his vision daylight coming through in great quantities and then the sliding glass doors at the front of the lobby. The mechanic whoosh sounded and the doors rolled their separate ways open before him. Cold air came forth and washed over his face as he walked out into the world and at last looked up.

There were rows of cars in the parking lot there. The morning was bright with the sun up a good distance above the horizon with no clouds in the pale blue sky. There were still many inches of snow on the landscape in those parts not traversed. The asphalt of the parking lot and the road leading out to the street were however bare. A thin line of water ran down the edge of the road abutting the curb and there were puddles about from the melting snow. The feeling came over Beau again that he should keep moving and he did, walking out to the cars of the parking lot, knowing that the truck would not be there.

As he walked the first aisle of this parking lot he spotted an older man walking out ahead. Beau sped up a bit, following him. The man reached into his pocket and brought out his keys and diverted off towards a small red car. Beau sped up his walk all the more as the man reached the driver's side door of this car and put his key into the lock by the handle.

"Excuse me!" Beau shouted out with some effort not to sound alarming.

The man did not hear and opened the door.

"Excuse me!" Beau said louder as he accelerated to a jog to quickly close the twenty or so feet between them.

This did catch the man's attention and he looked up in Beau's direction and saw him advancing toward him. Beau raised his hand and reduced his jog back to a walk. The man squinted with some curiosity.

"Thank you," Beau said. "Sorry, thank you."

Beau walked over to the side of the car as the man stood beside its open door with the keys in his hand and waiting.

"Yessir?" the man asked.

"Sorry. Thanks for stopping."

"Okay."

"Listen," Beau said, turning his sight back to where they had walked the parking lot and to the front doors of the medical center, as if he expected someone else to be there running after him. Finding no one there, Beau looked back to the man, which did further the puzzled glare upon the man's face. "Which way you heading?" Beau asked, with a bit of breath lost from the jog over, and with such breath appearing and then dissipating in the cold air.

"Me? I'm heading home."

"Where's home?"

"East. Out east of town."

"I'm sorry to be asking mister, would you mind giving me a lift?"

"Oh," the old man said, looking downward as if thinking of what he could say to alter the direction of where this abrupt conversation was taking them. But finding nothing there, he said "Well, where you heading?"

"Downtown."

The man looked at him a moment. "You ain't heard?"

"Heard?"

"You haven't heard whats happened?"

Beau put his hands to his hips.

"There isn't a downtown no more," the man said. "Whole damn thing's burned to the ground."

The man it seemed noticed the emblem at the center of Beau's cowboy hat and a realization came together upon his face. "Oh, sorry. I'm sorry. I, I wasn't tracking." The man swept his hand through the air and back toward the open door of the car. "Come on."

- Beau

One Sunday a while back, Reverend preached on the following from the book of the prophet Amos in regards to God's people Israel.

> I saw the Lord standing by the altar, and he said:
> Strike the tops of the pillars so that the thresholds shake.
> Bring them down on the heads of all the people;
> those who are left I will kill with the sword.
> Not one will get away, none will escape.
> Though they dig down to the depths below, from there my hand will take them.
> Though they climb up to the heavens above, from there I will bring them down.
> Though they hide themselves on the top of Carmel,
> there I will hunt them down and seize them.
> Though they hide from my eyes at the bottom of the sea,
> there I will command the serpent to bite them.
> Though they are driven into exile by their enemies,
> there I will command the sword to slay them.

I will keep my eye on them
for harm and not for good.

The Lord, the LORD Almighty—
he touches the earth and it melts,
and all who live in it mourn;
the whole land rises like the Nile,
then sinks like the river of Egypt;
he builds his lofty palace in the heavens
and sets its foundation on the earth;
he calls for the waters of the sea
and pours them out over the face of the
land—
the LORD is his name.

The passage struck me crosswise and set me to thought
for some time. So much so that I went down there and met
with Reverend about it. I said to him, I have never heard
anything so scary in all my life, to which Reverend nodded
in agreement. Puzzled that he did not elaborate, I
continued on and told him that God himself seemed to have
been the most terrifying thing in all the universe. Again he
nodded in apparent agreement without further explanation,
which did this time aggravate me some.

I said, I thought that God was supposed to be love.
Again, Reverend nodded, I gathered at this point to see how
far I would go down this line of thought until he saw just
where I stood. But I said nothing. Just looked at him and
shook my head. And that's where I stood.

He said, we must understand how vast are both God's wrath and His love. If we ignore His wrath, we will not understand His love, not in a right way. The two, they are connected, as are all His traits. Do you see, he asked me. I thought on it, but did not answer him.

Reverend began again, If you choose only to know His love, but not His holiness, and not His wrath, then son, you will not know Him at all. And I suspect you won't know yourself either. Can we know God? I asked. Reverend thought on that for a moment. Reverend said, those souls who claim that you can know everything about Him this side of heaven are indeed mistaken. But those who regard God as someone indiscernible are the most dangerous kind of fools, he said. Damn fools, he said. For He has spoken. Spoken and walked amongst us hisself. Reverend nodded to the Bible which lay on his desk. Reverend kept his gaze there until I was tracking.

Reverend said, When I start talking with a person about God, I always start with the wrath. Cause if a person is not ready to come to terms with it, the love is a thing irrelevant. For His love is first a salvation, which then extends out infinite to joys beyond what could be imagined. But if this person does not see first the predicament, and that His wrath extends out infinite the other direction, again, beyond what could be imagined, there is no place to begin. There is nothing yet to understand.

What about the cross, I asked. What about it, Reverend said. Wasn't that the end all of the wrath? I asked. Reverend's face turned grave. That cross, he said, that cross spoke as much about God's love for His children as it did about His fury for all their sins. He said, with his own

230

dead Son hanging on that tree, He left no doubt for the rest of the ages that He is as serious about His wrath as He is about His love.

Reverend then leaned in towards me across that desk and looked down through my eyes. He said, son, don't doubt His love. Don't doubt His wrath. For they are the both of them soaked in blood and we will all be swept up by one or the other when all is said and done. Sure as day we will.

Reverend leaned back again and was quiet a moment. He brought his hands together in contemplation as he looked at my face for some reaction. You're right you know, he said.

I sat quiet.

He is to be feared more than anything, Reverend said, now looking off into some space beside me. He ... is God. Even His love sets me to a shudder.

Beau asked that the man drop him off on a corner three blocks down from where Beau had parked the truck the night before at the edge of Main Street. The man was confused and offered to take him further to his truck, but Beau convinced him of the spot which he had requested and the man pulled over there and let him out. The stench of the place was strong of a sour haze like that of a forest fire. Beau looked around and did not see anyone walking around directly. Beau thanked the man. The man began an attempt to engage in some further conversation but Beau said goodbye to the man mid-sentence and walked away down the sidewalk, looking down the road.

Beau walked to the next street over running parallel and walked the three blocks down toward Main Street. He saw no one upon the street. The fire had not reached the row of structures here, though the stench of whatever the fire left behind grew stronger with each step. Beau saw out ahead the alleyway he had planned to use to cut over. He reached it and walked into the narrow opening and continued down the alleyway to its end at the road that would lead to the mouth of Main Street. He walked over close to the wall of the last building before the road and came at last to its corner. He leaned against the wall as he stuck his head out and looked down the road.

There was nothing left of those rows of buildings that had made up the heart of the town. Translucent waves of smoke rose all around from piles of charred debris and mess all down that block, with the devastation expanding outward at least three blocks to each of the street's sides. Many people walked around on Main Street itself. Three fire engines were parked in the center of the road bearing the emblems of foreign stations. A dozen or so law enforcement vehicles were parked on the street beside. These were also vehicles foreign to his office, with various officers standing around, most of which had no attachment to him. The carbonized skeleton of the fire engine that had burned during the conflict sat at Main Street's center like a hulking black corpse.

But there was his truck, fifty yards or so back from the beginnings of where all these people congregated, alongside a number of other cars left from the night. They might not see. They might not notice, he thought. There was no one on the sidewalk on this side of the street leading down to where his truck was parked. Without taking counsel of another thought he stepped out onto the sidewalk and walked quickly toward the truck.

Beau stared out at a spot some ten feet in front of him on the ground as he walked. He could not help but to hold his breath, and when he noticed this, he tried to let it go, which took him several steps before he was successful. His returning breath was short. He felt his heart hammering within. He reached the truck and unlocked it by pressing down the button upon the key fob and opened the driver side door and hopped in and shut it. He could not bring himself to look up to see who might be looking on as he maneuvered the key into the ignition. He turned on the truck and put it quick to reverse, though as with the medical room before, the thought occurred to him that it was necessary for the beginnings of this retreat to not have any added attention to it. He turned to look through the back window and slowly reversed, turning the truck as he did, so that his truck would wind up perpendicular to the road. He stopped, and with the patience that he could manage, he shifted the truck to drive, turned its nose the other direction, and slowly pulled away down the road.

Beau could feel the rush surging through his veins, opening his eyes wide, as his heart pounded and his breath became something audible. He heard nothing above the engine's soft whir as he continued to roll at a gradual pace entirely inconsistent with the terror that raced within him. After twenty seconds had passed, and the end of the road leading to the highway could be seen out ahead, Beau had to divert all the strength he could muster to bring himself to look at the rearview mirror. He shot a glance quickly to the rearview mirror, but the dread just as quickly pushed such glance back to the road.

Beau imagined that the whole crowd and authorities had screamed out collectively before rushing forth to their vehicles and making chase after him with sirens and engines and lights roaring, with such mob bearing down upon him at that moment. Beau closed his eyes and then opened them. He looked to the rear view mirror. There was nothing on the road behind him. Nothing at all. Except for a fog of smoke and mist out in the distance where downtown had once stood.

Beau drove on. When he reached a spot just before the onramp for the highway he pulled over to the side of the road and stopped. He was nauseous and thought he might vomit. Beneath all such feeling however was that pain for her. He sat with the engine idle and thought. She would not remain at home while he was in the hospital through the night. She would not. He thought on it more. He looked at the sign for the highway. The number "19" in a sterile white font atop a simple green. He stared at this number and reached out to her as it were, speaking to her within himself.

His vision came focused again upon the 19. A thought arose which forced his jaw rigid and biting down. As the thought settled, he diverted the force of this bite forward with his front teeth pushing down into his bottom lip until the pain matched the fears that this thought provoked. Beau stepped down upon the gas pedal. The truck spun out a bit and skidded leftwards before he corrected its path straight as it lurched forward. Beau got control of the thing and sped up the onramp to the highway. He accelerated rapidly and then merged onto the highway back out to the desert.

Susie drove the highway out to mile marker 115 and turned onto the service road as she thought that Beau would have. The snow upon the road was melting, though she saw clearly the tire tracks left from the night, confirming within herself that this was the way that he had come. She drove the two miles of the service road slow until she reached its end. She saw here more tire tracks from where his truck had parked and later spun out and turned around. She parked there and got out.

Susie looked out over the desert, out at the mesas in the distance, and over the sprawling plains enveloped in white. Their path, with its many prints, was clear still in the snow leading out toward the canyons past the horizon. She thought about what Beau must have found at the end of this path and what would be there still.

She opened the passenger side door of her small pickup and retrieved her winter coat and put it on. She brought the hood up over her head. She got out also snow boots from the cab and sat down on the edge of the open cab door and removed her sneakers. She put the boots on and tucked her jeans inside their tops. She stood up, closed the door, and looked back out to the world that awaited. She put her hands into the pockets of the jacket and set out on the path.

The snow still covered the entirety of the desert around her, its brightness reflecting the sun at full strength, making her squint. She trudged through the snow on the path, looking downwards mostly at the prints that remained in the snow, which were losing their form from the morning. Though she could not tell which of these prints had been her husband's, she knew that many were, which comforted her some.

She looked over the plains. At those tan and red mesa heads that bore the snow in various places as if pearl decoration. She shook her head at the beauty of what had been made around her. She said aloud, "You are good."

As she looked out upon the skinny path that cut through such world, she thought that many would be afraid of where it would lead. Though when she thought on it more, she concluded that people are only scared of the ends of the paths that they are on if they are scared of who they are. She knew it was right that she was not afraid. For her life was not her own, and had not been for some time.

After she had walked in the quiet with which the Lord had filled that place for a half hour, her mind turned to the word, and eventually to Job. Job's story was hidden in her heart for her there. She ran his story in her mind. And she said aloud, "Naked I came to the world. Naked I will leave it. Blessed be the Lord."

She thought about Moses and his plagues. She looked to the blue of the sky and imagined it filled with swirling black masses of locusts like mountains in the air. The whir of a trillion wings together like thunder.

She thought of Noah. The deeps tearing like paper and pouring forth the blood of the earth until that is all that was and there was no more.

She thought about the night the angel of the Lord struck down 185,000 Assyrians. And His people awoke to find their corpses stretched to the horizon. The birds and beasts that must have descended by the thousands upon them. She knew the terror wrought from our sins is a story as old as time and has always been made of events unthinkable that prove men small.

She stopped walking. She saw out far ahead something on the ground. It was not moving. The trail of prints in the snow would lead her directly to it. Out past this thing a distance was the lip of the canyon, with just the tops of its gulf visible from the angle.

The snow and ice on the highway had melted with the morning and Beau was driving 90 miles per hour as he approached the mile marker. The tires screeched with the moisture and the truck shook as he stepped the brake down hard to make the turn off to the service road. The rear tires skidded out in the turn and he had to bring the entire truck to a stop so as to return control, nearly sliding off the top of the service road down its sloped side to the shoulder three feet below. The gravel based road stretched out before him and still bore snow upon it, though it appeared as not much more formed than a slush. Beau shifted on the four-wheel high. The truck jerked forward and jolted his head back as he stomped back down on the gas pedal, quickly making it up to a speed just beyond what he felt in control.

Susie kept her eyes on this thing laid out on the ground during her entire approach to it. There was a turn in her lower stomach, subtle, but consistent and present. When she was within thirty yards she knew it to be a body. She could now make out a halo of some dark substance surrounding it upon the earth. She braced for the sight of it and continued.

She raised her hand to cover her mouth involuntarily as she reached him. The throat and lower half of his face had been crushed completely up to the nose and had burst. His

237

eyes were half open and bloodshot, looking at her and then past her as she walked up and then stood over him. She knew it was Coleman. Her heart filled with a pain and a pity which could be felt as if from an actual wound. She kept her hand over her mouth as she continued to look down upon him. The sight of him was true, as she knew, though her mind fought to reject it as a foreign thing too strange to be part of the world. There was no peace to him, but only a rawness and a violence that could never be removed. A crooked stain upon the earth.

She stepped carefully around the edges of the blood and fluid that had frozen around him like a syrup atop the snow, which had melted and sunk such snow around him at first before freezing and texturing a jagged ice around him. She tried her best to step quietly while walking around and past him, as if it would have been an offense to have disturbed the message that the scene was speaking to the world. As she made it past him several feet she turned her eyes back to the path which continued on, speaking to herself in her mind that this was the path of others as well as her own, and that they too each had their truths written upon it. When she looked out now, it was not more than a couple hundred yards to reach the point where the surface dropped away. There was another body that could be seen out upon such edge, and it too was upon the ground, though part of it was upright.

The sight of her pickup parked at the end of the service road was the worst thing Beau had ever seen. Though he had begged within his heart for the past half hour that it would not be so, he had known from the moment the thought entered his mind back in town that this was happening, as if it were not a thought, but the sound of the pen, making it so, and the momentum of the whole thing at its terminal point before the impact.

Beau slowed the truck with a skid as he pulled in next to hers, parallel and facing out to the desert. The noses of both trucks were pointed directly down the line of tracks that all involved had left while traveling out to the horizon. His mind turned as he sat. She could not be seen. The thought occurred to him that what he feared could already be a part of the world. She could be gone. That very moment. She could have come out here hours ago. He searched not his mind but his heart, reaching out to unknown places to feel if it were so. He could still feel her. Beau shifted the truck back to drive and drove out onto the path. The truck slid back and forth, one direction, then the other, but forward and moving some twenty miles per hour toward her.

The man was sitting on the edge of the canyon, with his legs hanging over its lip, staring out at the expanse and the layers of earth imperfectly stacked and falling to the base far below. She stopped walking about twenty feet out from him and stood there. She had known that he knew she was there from the time she first spotted him out ahead. He was sitting still, and though she could not tell exactly from her angle directly behind him, it seemed as if he rested his hands upon his lap. The whole scene was like a painting, with all the beauty of the world natural and composing most all the canvas, and this foreign thing, this counterfeit observer, dropped in the middle of the depiction to make a point like a grotesque contradiction, though the details of the point were for the onlooker to decide.

The man twisted his body and head in a lean to see her. He looked at her for a moment without much expression to his face and then turned back to look out over the canyon again. She walked toward him, seeing now the end of the footprints that stopped before him in what felt an abrupt conclusion. She came within just feet of him and stopped. His dark hair glistened with a moisture down his bare back.

"Do you think he will understand?" the man asked.

"Yes."

The man thought. "That doesn't mean that he deserves you though. Does it?"

Susie was quiet for a moment. She stepped forward and bent down to sit beside the man on the edge, being careful to keep control from slipping over until she was settled. She looked out at what the man saw. The drop which filled the canyon invoked the feeling of danger, but it was quieted by the purity of the beauty all about it which extended outwards until the world was small, and then upwards to the pale heavens.

"Isn't that the point?" she asked.

The man nodded his head. "To reject such a thing on his behalf would be far worse even than the choices that required it."

"It's the kindness in paying for what is required that makes the requirement at last undeniable, along with everything else."

The man looked to her as if pleased to be continually surprised by her and then turned his eyes back to the scene. "To some," he said.

She thought about this. "It will be to him. I have not a doubt."

"All right."

"It's the end of all this," she said.

"Who could deny the precedent?"

A soft drone could be heard behind them. Susie turned back. She saw Beau's truck a mile out and speeding toward them, spraying a mist all about.

"Can I ask you something?" she asked, turning back to the man

The man remained quiet.

"Is this what you wanted? All along?"

The man nodded, accepting the question as worthwhile. "I had nothing particular in mind. Only the admission." He looked to her. "Though the more I saw of him, the more I saw all the world. And you, I saw in you all that I did not see in him." The man looked back out. "The thought did occur to me that it would be you in the end."

It was quiet between them as the sound of the engine grew steadily.

"You know," the man began again, "if he would have left me in that box his father put me in, none of this would have happened." The man sighed. "All these people." The man looked to her. "But he would have still been the same man. The very same. He would just have been able to shut his eyes to it for the rest of whatever life he was allowed." The man again looked away, not at all concerned about the sound of the engine which continued to build.

"You said nothing to tempt him?"

"Not a word. Truth is, people have a multitude of cages down in the dark of themselves and they open them all given enough time. And no fear about it at all."

"And you thought it your place to teach us."

The man thought about this a moment.

"Teach? No. But there was a point when I was down there in that dark, after a long while, that I did resolve to make it plain to at least one of you hypocrites that the things that you do, that you fill this world with, all of it, they look just – like – me."

The sound of the tires peeling on the snow could now also be heard clear under the roar of the engine.

"Who is the murderer?" the man asked again. "These people murder all the world."

The man slid himself back away from the edge and pushed himself up to his knees and then up to standing over her. "You sure this is what you want?"

The engine was blaring now. The sound of it cut out as the tires squealed atop the snow until the truck was stopped. Beau had stopped the truck some fifty yards back from where they stood at the canyon's edge. The door of the truck could be heard opening and then Beau's voice yelling.

Susie also slid herself back and brought herself up to standing beside the man, looking to his eyes.

"He's had every chance," the man said.

"Susie!" Beau yelled out as he ran now toward them. "Get back! Get away from him!"

Susie stared at the man's eyes for a moment longer. She then turned to Beau, who was screaming and running toward her. She kept her eyes set upon him, a gentle face amidst all the noise, and she stepped back carefully three steps until she felt the very edge underneath her foot.

"Stop!" Beau screamed. "Susie!" Beau was now fifteen yards away on a sprint and looked not at the man to her side but only to her face. She smiled at him. She raised her arms to be outstretched on each side and was still but for a half-second. She then leaned backwards and fell from view.

"Susie!" he screamed again, running and stumbling and falling onto his chest, sliding on the snow right up to the edge and looking over. She fell fast, her arms flailing from the force of the wind pushing back up upon her, but not with panic. It was two seconds before she was but a falling form, shrinking and pulling away from him until she was small. This tiny form met with the ground far below and moved no more.

Beau screamed out with all that was in his lungs down into the canyon toward her until his voice gave out. His scream filled the place and echoed about and then faded until it was gone. Though she was a small thing there below, with no detail visible, he saw that she laid with outstretched arms to her sides in the same position she had put herself before the fall. The pain was physically hot within him and it made him shake throughout his body. He let his face fall to the snow at the edge there and shut his eyes tight. He pushed his face into the snow as hard as he could. The frost burned all it touched on his face. He could still see her, lying there, and knew that this would be what he saw always. He screamed again into the snow, with the slush pushing up into his mouth and choking out the cry. He rolled to his side and put both his hands upon the center of his chest from where the pain flowed and kept them there and laid still. There was a low buzz in his ears as if from a noise that had erupted beside him. This ring held constant. He cried out again in the pain.

Beau opened his eyes to the sky above. A soft blue. Extending upward forever.

He sat up. He looked all around, at first at the area close about him, then extending outward across the void of the barren desert plains beyond, blanketed and shining in a white pure that man did not, and cannot, create. He was alone. Utterly alone. This world, massive in ways far beyond what people are able to perceive. And him, a thing microscopic within it. Though that soul within his chest, if seen true, would make the whole of the earth a thing insignificant by its comparison. That soul is eternal, and will exist in a time so far removed from when such world burns away, that this world itself will be seen then only as a moment, a thought. Trivial. The whole place a short-lived stage for such souls to reveal their allegiances and the destinies assigned. And the whole thing dangling above the oblivion.

He thought – all such space, and all such weight, and all such substance – nothing. She but a speck in this mass unimaginable, and yet was its purpose entire. Torn and gone. That woman.

THE END

Acknowledgements

Zachary would like to express his gratitude to the family and friends that supported him and read the draft manuscripts leading to this final work. Zachary would like to express particular gratitude to Rebecca Donofrio, a talented author herself, who edited this book with much effort and care through several reviews.

About the Author

Zachary is a native of New Mexico and of the greater Southwest, growing up surrounded by those desert lands, with open space and mesas and canyons and rugged mountain terrain stretching out beyond the horizon. A wide open stage with space for big stories. Zachary is drawn to many kinds of literature, but has been especially influenced by the work of Cormac McCarthy, and in particular, Blood Meridian and his Border Trilogy. Zachary is also a music junkie, and is constantly inspired by musicians from all genres. *They Are Only Men* is Zachary's first novel.